T0129294

TALKING
WITH HORSES

TALKING WITH HORSES

... IN LOVE AND WAR

COLIN DANGAARD

TALKING WITH HORSES
... IN LOVE AND WAR

iUniverse books may be ordered through booksellers or by contacting:

iUniverse
1663 Liberty Drive
Bloomington, IN 47403
www.iuniverse.com
1-800-Authors (1-800-288-4677)

ISBN: 978-1-5320-7835-4 (sc)
ISBN: 978-1-5320-7836-1 (e)

Print information available on the last page.

iUniverse rev. date: 12/27/2019

PRELUDE

This is a love story and it happens in the hills of Malibu, California. A beautiful young college student with autism unwittingly uses her condition to communicate with her horse in a way that was common between humans and horses millions of years ago. For Emma, it happens as naturally as breathing. Other modern people can also communicate like this today, but for most it is difficult, requiring training and concentration that is rare. The brain of modern man mantles his oldest brain – a cerebral structure that performs the primary functions in autism. This is Emma's story. And how she finds love with a troubled young man, in real time, and with a Lieutenant of Attila the Hun in her autistic fantasy. She is a warrior at his side, in bloody conflicts with the Romans. Emma's Hun lover saves her life, and she saves his life. This is also the story of the evolution of the horse – and how man and horse learned to communicate.

To horses and all the people they love

Special thanks to the International Museum of the Horse, Lexington, Kentucky, for unbridled support – especially Director Bill Cook and Curatorial Assistant Shannon Leva

FOREWORD

Colin Dangaard is not one put off by a challenge – not even telling the story of the horse through a mystical collection of characters like a jumping horse named Tower, an autistic girl named Emma, the Vikings, and Attila the Hun. All this while Emma falls in love with Zehun, a fantasy lieutenant of Attila the Hun, as she romances Jules, a handsome young man in real life, and *then* saves the family's Malibu horse ranch. *Talking with Horses* will change forever the way you think of a horse. For more on Colin's story, check the back of this book!
Bill Reynolds
Santa Ynez, California

Colin's book is the most unique and innovative insight into human and horse interaction of my acquaintance … a fascinating landmark.
Henry Curry, MD

Colin Dangaard is an expert – saddlemaker, businessman, entrepreneur, journalist, and horseman. If you're a horse lover, mule lover, or just casually interested in horses, get ready for an interesting and enlightening "ride" through this book. Colin uses all his senses, experience, and knowledge gathered through many years as a true student of equine to carry his readers through the fascinating and mesmerizing world of equine communication and history. His ability to weave all of his experience into a fascinating story makes this book one I guarantee will keep you up late at night reading and wanting more.

Dr. Jerry Johnson
Head of Psychology
West Michigan State University

This book has touched my heart greatly for the special needs children who are *highly medicated* because nobody wants to take the time to figure a more natural way. I am the mother of a special needs son, who is actually brilliant, but "different" compared with what people would call "normal." Emma's connection with her horse puts her in a natural place where she feels secure, safe, and understood. This is a story that reminds me to listen to my inner self. It has inspired me to connect more closely with my own horse *Gracie*, who is empowering me and thereby helping me be inspired by my gifted, but different, son Zac.

Susan Williams
Westlake, California

Talking with Horses – I couldn't put it down. It has inspired me to open a facility using horses to help kids with autism and other brain problems.

Ken Glaser
Nowthren, Minnesota

Horse lovers and history lovers are in for a treat with this amazing book!

Chris Davies, Australia

CHAPTER ONE

Sunday, January 17, 2010. The Santa Monica Mountains, California. A full moon, silhouetting rugged cliffs against a clear night sky. Emma Armbrust could read right now – if she had a book. She is riding her seventeen-hand horse Tower, a thoroughbred, with Man O' War breeding on both sides. Emma Armbrust is eighteen years old, the horse ten years – which in human years makes Tower forty. Emma often thinks about this and marvels at how Tower doesn't feel that old. Tower rotates one ear back in her direction, and she smiles; he knows what she is thinking. She had projected an image of a very old swaybacked horse.

Emma pats his neck and says, "There now. I think you're just as young as you feel."

The ear rotates back to a forward position. Tower is okay with that thought.

"Come on," she says, "let's gallop up this hill. I know you hate to walk uphill."

She does not kick him or use the crop. She simply leans forward, ever so slightly, so her body does not whip back as Tower leaps into a flat gallop. But *even before she leans forward, she knows he knows what she is thinking.* He tells her this feels really good as the hill slips beneath at breathtaking speed. Tower's hooves are muffled on earth softened by heavy rain. Like a dancer, he carefully negotiates deep ruts caused by running water. Fifteen minutes later, they crest the ridge on the top of a mesa, the sky so close it seems to Emma she could reach out and touch it.

Emma feels Tower's heart beating between her legs as he sucks in vast amounts of air. His nostrils flare like trumpets. His hot breath frosts the night. Way down in the valley below, Emma sees the lights of her father's horse farm, where Tower was bred to race. But despite his impressive heritage, he was slow. Years later, when Tower was six years old and Emma thirteen, she started riding him, having given up her pony Nugget.

Tower told her that he wasn't slow at all; he just didn't like the competition, didn't like racing against his friends in the way people wanted. He was okay with racing as play but not as work. He liked to jump, which he did at every opportunity. Several times he jumped out of the paddock, until Emma told him to quit doing that or he would be "sent down the road." She overheard her father tell the stable hand, Manuel, as much. Emma didn't like Manuel, and Tower liked him even less. Because Tower couldn't run fast enough to win, Manuel considered him "dog food in search of a can."

Tower does not have the direct communication with Manuel that exists between him and Emma, because Manuel cannot read the pictures in Tower's head the way Emma can. Between Tower and Emma, the images are crystal clear, going both ways. With these pictures, words are not necessary; indeed, they hinder. At most, they are tools of exclamation or embellishment. This is how it was millions of years ago between man and horse. And this is how it is today between Emma and Tower. Few people today have this power of extraordinary communication. Most who do are to varying degrees autistic.

Emma studies the ground. The print is still there: a mountain lion. She saw it yesterday afternoon. Judging by the size of the paw print, the lion is about 250 pounds. Tower is completely disinterested. He knows the lion is long gone. He has picked up its electromagnetic energy. The image in Tower's mind, which he knows Emma is receiving now, is of a lioness way over the north ridge.

Suddenly Tower freezes and looks up at the moon, his body trembling. Emma follows his riveted concentration, and then sees what Tower sees. It is as if her body is drawn up through the tunnel of light that is her gaze. The image has clear edges, and it cuts up into the night sky. At the end, there is a very bright light that seems to draw Emma up, moving her at ever-increasing speed, until she is overwhelmed by the dense brightness. Cracking thunder and lightning split the night sky, as if disemboweling the heavens. Rain drives down on Emma, drops so large they feel like rocks flying into her face.

Solid ground is under her feet now. The air is filled with screaming, blood everywhere, as a horde of mounted horsemen bear down on a small village. All around her, death and pain and terrible agony. Emma is flat on the ground now, slammed down by a massive force, and one of the savages crashes upon her, tearing at her deerskin garment, pulling at her hair. She is overcome with the raw, rotten stench of his breath; it smells of blood. The night is swirling around her, as if she is lost in a whirlpool of black water, being sucked down, down. Women and children scream, a background to the pain and thunder and driving, hard rain. The man is on top of Emma now, his eyes blazing into her soul. Then he throws back his head and screams like a hyena, the sound piercing Emma's ears.

Emma knows she is going to die, but then, suddenly she sees him. A tall man, appearing as a rising backdrop behind her attacker, his skin, not black, not white – a golden brown. His chest is bare, except for a gold amulet hanging from his neck.; veins pumped like whipcords, sweat glistening off muscles rippled across his torso and down his massive arms. She locks eyes with this man behind the monster, and his eyes stop her heart, as they always did. Oh yes, it's him all right. She has seen him before, many times. The eyes glow green. His face is finely chiseled, black hair pulled back and tied with a leather thong. Emma is aware of a bloody sword in his hand as he grabs her attacker by the hair, pulls back his head, and draws his sword across the monster's throat – stretched and vulnerable, perfectly angled for a clean, deep slash – like a bow pulled across strings of a musical instrument, a closing symphony of death.

Emma feels a red-hot gush on her face. She locks eyes with this man who has saved her, his great frame now completely visible, as the savage is flung aside like a bloody rag doll. He smiles, his teeth brilliant and white in the moonlight. He leans forward, wipes her face, his hands strong but incredibly soft and warm. The hands cup Emma's head, and the warrior asks, "You are all right?" She hears his words so clearly, although all around them is earsplitting chaos – screaming, clanging of swords, the animal-like bellowing of bloodthirsty savages, and the driving rain, the sky hemorrhaging thunder and lightning. This man locks eyes with her one more time for what seems like forever, but is in fact an instant; his green eyes deliver a burning beam of light that goes deep into Emma's soul.

Emma looks past the green eyes now, and there is a new horror, another warrior, with sword raised, a giant of a man, with leopard skin over his head, and he is screaming not at Emma, but at the man with the green eyes, "Why haven't you killed her? She is a worthless piece of meat! We have raided this village to kill, kill!"

In a flash, the man with green eyes ducks low and swings his sword upward, sending the sword from the hand of Leopard Man rattling off into the storm. Now Leopard Man is defenseless, his eyes wide with fear. And then the man with the green eyes puts his sword at the throat of Leopard Man and says, "I rank above you with Attila! Never try that again, or you will die. We are warriors, not savages. We kill other warriors. We do not kill the defenseless! This girl lives ..."

Leopard Man growls and spits, "You are soft. You are not a real killer. Attila will hear about this!"

And then, the vision fades, and now Emma is shivering. She opens her eyes, relief flooding over her. She is so thankful to be sitting now on Tower, here in the hills of Malibu, the night suddenly blanketed in deep silence. Her heartbeat slows, her whole being shaken by those piercing eyes.

Emma is calm but confused. She has seen this man many times before, but always in her dreams – her "vision time," as she privately thinks of it. This was the first time she had seen the vision in her "awake" time. She composes herself and sucks in the cool air. Tower snorts and tells her he is fine too. Oh yes, he witnessed the battle, because Emma had seen it and, as usual, shared the pictures. For Tower, the horror of it has also passed. He is ready now for Emma's command.

Emma's cell phone rings, shrill and strange in this setting. It's her father, Allan. Yes, she tells him, she's coming home now. Even while talking with her father, words are difficult. It's like she is playing over a recorded response, because she knows he, too, cannot communicate in pictures. He cannot transmit them, cannot receive them. He uses words.

Early in life, Emma learned a name for the "condition" that made her so different: autism. People with this condition, she would learn, have communication patterns reflecting the world as seen through the eyes of another, older brain – in her case, the horse. Everything is processed in pictures, transmitted by an energy she knows is there, but cannot explain. Emma does not understand how this happens. She is simply comforted with the fact that it does happen and that it always has happened, naturally, comfortably. The world of words is her challenge. The world of pictures is her home.

Before she can holster the cell phone, Tower turns and heads down the hill, toward home. There will be no more galloping tonight. As her father always said – "gallop out from the barn, but walk home." Tower never argues. He hates being put away wet. There are no more images. Tower thinks only of food. Emma thinks about school the next day, Monday. She likes school, but she doesn't sound like the other girls. They call her "Miss Geek" and "retard." They say she talks "funny," which prompts another name – "tape recorder."

Of course, they are right. Emma's tone is flat. But she doesn't know why. With Tower she does not need words, making talking with him so easy! Communication with her friends has an odd warp, like sounds coming up from a tunnel. Even when she understands the words, they are mixed, often rendering sentences unintelligible. She mostly guesses what has been said. The message is not always clear and is thus very frustrating. Reading lips helps. But with Tower, everything is perfectly clear. Images she receives from him have clear edges, like cut glass. She understands everything he is thinking, as clearly as if she were looking at a silent movie. She doesn't know why others cannot see these pictures. To Emma it is so obvious. But strangely, knowing why is not important. For Emma, Tower is the perfect companion, always there, always loving, never judging her. He is her gentle giant.

CHAPTER TWO

Night, Sunday, January 17. The gate to the Armbrust farm is open, just as Emma had left it earlier in the afternoon. The moon is clouding, but she finds the electric gate switch. She closes the gate for the night. She rides into the barn, where the light has been left on. There are ten stalls on each side of the great wooden structure. Each stall is occupied, except for the one on the end, which is Tower's stall. The horses greet each other as usual, heads reaching over half-doors, hooves pawing, lips slapping, noisy muffling sounds. They want to know where Tower has been, what he has been doing, but he ignores them. Of course, they are each reaffirming their place in the pecking order. Emma always wonders why Tower is not the leader. Among ten horses he is the least important. He was in the same last position when the ranch had twenty horses. Emma does not know how they establish this order; she just knows they do. And it is very clear. No horse ever steps out of the order unless one horse is removed, thus opening up a new space higher up – or lower. Tower will share with them all images later, at his leisure. Right now, he wants food!

Emma secures Tower in the crossties, tells him to be still, and then pulls off her Australian stock saddle – the only saddle her father lets her ride on the trail, especially if she is alone.

Emma places the saddle on the rack now and spreads the sweat-soaked "numnah" on top. The numnah is cut from a single Merino sheepskin to fit the shape of the saddle, hair side down. Tomorrow it will be dry, and before Emma puts it back on the horse, she will brush out the sweat balls. Her father had left the tack-room light on, and Emma catches a glimpse of herself in a dusty mirror. She has a bad case of "helmet hair," but there is still a freshness and bounce to her long golden locks falling casually down slender shoulders. She decides, looking at herself, that she has a beauty that pleases her – well-defined cheeks, deep blue eyes, a large generous mouth, dimples, and flawless, cream-colored skin. She turns and considers her breasts. She is happy with those as well. She has become acutely aware that boys look at her breasts before they make eye contact. It used to annoy her. She felt like she had to duck to make eye contact with them. But recently she has started to consider it flattering.

She hears Tower calling and realizes she has forgotten to feed him.

"Okay," she says apologetically.

She hurries out, fills his bucket with four-way grain and alfalfa replacer pellets, dumps it in his feed bin, and leads him into his stall. "Sorry, I was daydreaming." Tower pays her no mind and buries his nose in his feed. For a while, Emma stays there, empty bucket in hand, sharing his joy. He turns his rump toward her, as if cutting her off from his food. He sends no pictures. "Okay," she says, "sorry!"

"Hey, Emma," the voice of her dad comes from outside, "who's in there with you?"

"Tower," she says.

Allan is now in the circle of light. He is a squarely built man, at age 55, once wiry and muscled, but now taking on the easy look of middle age. He was always too heavy to be a jockey – okay for horse exercising – but fine to be the great horseman he was.

Allan laughs. "So you think he's talking to you!"

Emma is at once surprised and amused. "Yes, he talks me."

Allan rolls his eyes. "You're tired, girl. Time to go to bed."

Emma checks the horses one last time. Allan has turned off the tack-room light. Father and daughter stroll in silence up to the big house.

Emma eats supper, showers, goes into her room, and flops onto the bed, content in her space. The room is filled with pictures of horses. One shelf is lined with trophies won at Malibu Trancas Riders and Ropers, shrimp division through teens. She loves her room. Directly above her bed, pasted on the ceiling, is a large picture of her, age eleven, jumping Tower over three-foot rails down at the Trancas Arena. It was the first time she had jumped in a show. She had practiced only one day. She had set up a two-foot jump at home, took Tower up to it, and asked him to jump. As usual, she sent Tower a picture of him jumping smoothly, with her sitting perfectly in the saddle. He looked to the right, then left, then right again, and Emma knew what he was thinking. He wanted to go around the jump. He was confused. Why go over it, when there was so much room to go around? The picture he sent to Emma was of him strolling nonchalantly, circling the jump, kind of proud that he had thought of a much easier way to get to the other side of the jump.

"Jumping, this is what I want," she told him flashing another picture of him jumping and her riding him. "I know it is easier to go around, but this is what I want." Tower pointed his ears at the jump. He got the picture. Emma wondered why words came more easily when she was talking alone with Tower. But she knew he would jump because she had asked him to jump and she had transmitted a picture of him jumping. After that moment, for all time forward, he would take every jump without argument. At least with Emma aboard!

At the other end of the hallway now, in the sprawling old farmhouse, Allan and his wife, Millie, are curled up in bed. Millie is 20 years younger than Allan, a short cheerful woman with a ready laugh. She is watching old movies on Turner Broadcasting.

Allan waits until the movie is over, and then he says, "You know Emma is still talking to horses."

Millie looks at him, mocking surprise. "So? People talk to horses all the time. I talk to my dogs."

"Yeah," says Allan, "I know. No problem with that. What I have a problem with is she says the horses are talking to *her.* Now that is plain crazy."

"Well, maybe they are. I know what my dogs are thinking when they look at me."

"If she is hearing voices," says Allan, "we have a problem."

"You're overreacting. It's a stage young girls go through. It's normal. You remember that article I read, and I told you about it … about how young girls get anthropomorphic about their horses?"

"Now, what the hell does that mean?"

"It means they think of them as having human attributes. They treat them like humans. People do it with animals all the time."

They fall silent, husband and wife, and then Millie says quietly, "And, of course, bear in mind that Emma is mildly autistic."

"Yeah, well, they did say mild."

"Okay, but she is … still autistic."

Allan shakes his head. "Yeah, yeah. Heard it. Got it!"

"And this," Millie continues, "this might have something to do with her building a secure world within the world she knows. A world around her horse. Not people. And I know she visits a whole fantasy world exclusive to her."

"Now that," Allan says flatly, "is a bunch of psychobabble bullshit!"

Millie sits bolt upright in bed. "So now you're a psychologist? You can't even train a horse to race! Horses have been doing that for millions of years! What are we down to now? Five horses!"

Allan purses his lips and falls silent, and Millie feels a pang of regret. She should not have gone there, should not have said that. Allan is displeased with his record as a horse trainer. Only five good wins in fifteen years, causing financial hardship.

"Look," she says, "I love you and know you try your best for all of us. Let's talk about this tomorrow."

After a while, she continues in her soothing voice, "Sleep, my husband. Besides, we have more to worry about. Like how to pay the bills this month. Ever since you bought this horse ranch, it's been going downhill. Maybe you should get a job. I mean, a real job."

"That new colt, Blazing Light, he's gonna change all that."

"In your dreams!"

More silence, then Millie changes her tone. "Hey, here's another news flash for you. I hear Jules is back."

This causes Allen to sit bolt upright. "You're kidding me. Jules Chamberlaine? I thought he stayed back East to live with his dad after he got out of that correctional place."

"Yeah, well, that didn't work out. His dad went off the rails, and Jules got into more trouble. They sent him back to Juvenile Hall. Now he's out again, but this time he's back with his mother in Malibu."

"Does Emma know he's back?"

"Don't know. Don't think so. He came in just a couple of days ago."

"They spent a lot of time together as kids, Jules and Emma. I sure hope she has erased him from her memory. That's all we need, some ex-con with designs on our daughter!"

Now Millie is bolt upright. "Give him a break. He was a juvenile. From what I understand, you were no model kid in the Outback. Anyhow, maybe Jules has grown up. As you will recall he was – *is* – very smart. A history buff. All he did was read books about the history of the horse and all those warriors from the Dark Ages. Emma loved it when he read those stories to her when they were kids. They say Jules has a genius IQ."

"Yeah, well, so much for IQ. I know people with IQs that read like phone numbers, and they couldn't brush their teeth and listen to music at the same time. In my book, IQ means *In Question!*"

"Jules, he's a good kid," Millie offers. "Rough start, that's all."

"He was also weird. Never talked. Looked at his feet when you talked to him. A shifty-eyed little bastard. They never grow out of it, you know. He's got the gene, a touch of the dark side, a touch of the tar brush. And *that* gene is trouble. He's in a bad place, half white, half black. Neither black nor white!"

Millie turns and looks at him in wonderment. "You should hear yourself! This is the twenty-first century!"

"I have my opinions. Still a free country."

"And you're more than just a little racist."

Allan grunts.

Then, as if on an afterthought, Millie says, "I am convinced, by the way, that Emma and Tower communicate with each other as easily as you and I communicate. Perhaps even better, given the poor way you and I sometimes manage. Don't know how it happens, but it happens. Something to do with electromagnetic current produced by the brain. This is what I have read. Looked it up on the Internet."

Allan sighs, but is silent. He has heard this before. *One day, he promises himself, he's going to learn how to turn on the computer.*

Millie continues, "I remember you telling me stories about the wild Australian aboriginals who lived on your family's cattle property, and how they could communicate with each other over hundreds of miles, no telephones, and how you all thought that was perfectly natural."

"Yeah, well, that's true. But they were savages, after all. Just one step up from animals. I'm not saying animals don't communicate with each other, animal to animal. I'm saying it's not possible for people to converse with animals – at least, I see no evidence of it. Same as we can't mate with them!"

Millie stares at him. "Are you saying the Australian aboriginals you grew up with on your property were not people?"

"If you saw what I saw, you wouldn't think they were people either. They were not civilized like us. They didn't even wear clothes, for God's sake. They killed each other. That same thing they had going with communication, they could use it to kill somebody. Always some weirdo in the mob with the power to 'point the bone,' and when that happened, it was lights out. Best medicine in the world couldn't save an Abo from that!"

Millie laughs. "History is full of very civilized people who have killed each other – with or without their clothes on."

Millie is about to add another thought when she hears Allan snoring.

CHAPTER THREE

Allan Armbrust came to America from what he called "the old country" – Australia. He was born on a cattle property, Mulligan Station, in North Queensland, May 5, 1955, the first of three boys born two years apart. He was smaller than his brothers, but because he was the eldest, they never pushed him around. Allan had blond hair and blue eyes and, as his father always said, "more opinions than God." Allan left home after many knockdown fights with his father, who disagreed with just about everything Allan did – or didn't do.

At age fourteen, Allan joined a group of drovers who moved cattle 250 miles south to the small town of Battle Creek, where the cattle were sold and Allan was supposed to go to school. School didn't happen. He was expelled at the final year of grade school. Allan started working racehorses at the local track. Every Outback town had a racetrack. He also rounded up horses that had been let loose by the drovers and formed great brumby herds on the outskirts of town. The drovers had no further use for them – plenty more where they came from. The men camped at the sale yards, went into town, stayed drunk for a week, then threw their gear into a four-wheel-drive truck and returned to their cattle stations, only to repeat the whole process two months later. Allan found the drovers' horses easy to catch and sold these to tobacco farmers who couldn't afford tractors, and to parents of kids wanting ponies. At this time Australia was importing boatloads of immigrants from Italy, Greece, Northern Europe – any place that had men under 30 looking for a new life from the ravages of war. In World War 11, Australia lost more men per head of population than any other country. After all the fighting was over, Australia was a country of women and old men. The Government gave the immigrants land, jobs and money to get started and, as they became successful, their women followed. Young Allan Armbrust became more than a person of interest to Battle Creek law enforcement as he launched a career selling horses to which he did not hold title. Some were branded. The Battle Creek stock inspector called that horse stealing. Allan saw them only as "brumbies," feral horses he caught by stealing giant rolls of toilet paper from small rail motor sidings and stringing the paper on trees into a giant V, with an opening 100 yards across and leading up into a blind canyon. The horses shied off the white paper and were easily trapped. There he left them for three days without water or food, so they became "calm." While this was happening, he read books and wrote short stories, and lived on goannas he speared out of trees, and fish he caught in streams nearby. It was easy living. He sold the horses to impoverished tobacco farmers for what it would take a man a week to earn. All was well, until a drunken drover saw his favorite horse pulling a tobacco farmer's cart in Battle Creek. The farmer said he had paid a kid in the bush for the horse. And so the stock inspector began the hunt for a horse thief. Allan began to re-design his business model, but knew his lucrative game in the bush was running out of options.

At 139 pounds back then, he was light enough to exercise racehorses. He also started boxing, and did well when Jimmy Sharman and his Troupe came to town during the Battle Creek Rodeo. Jimmy's boxers would stand up on the platform in front of the big tent, in the divisions of lightweight, middleweight, and heavyweight, and fight any and all contenders. Allan fought lightweight. Every time he went three rounds, he collected $5.

He fought every day the Troupe was in town. His last fight, Allan went to his corner with a cut over his left eye, lid rapidly falling. The referee wanted to stop the fight, but Allan begged him not to. Jimmy Sharman's own "cut" man taped the top lid with an elastic bandage. "Good for a couple of minutes," said the cut man. Allan could blink, though barely. It worked. Allan won the fight, unleashing a brawling volley of punches. He left the ring with his eye completely shut. He never fought again, and instead worked racehorses every morning, starting at 4:00 a.m., and then took work on many cattle stations west and north of Battle Creek.

When he was twenty-six, he moved to America, fascinated with stories he had heard about horses and cattle there. Figured he could "show the Yanks a thing or two," being from the Outback. He went first to Florida and then to Texas, where he met and married Millie, the daughter of a schoolteacher, and then to California, where he continued training horses. Emma was born in Los Angeles, November 2, 1992, and grew up on the Malibu horse ranch that Allan purchased after a string of very good bets and some lucky real estate in Texas.

Over the years, Allan mended the emotional fences with his dad, who actually visited him twice in Texas and once in California. Allan never returned to Mulligan Station, and the 500 square miles was eventually sold for pennies on the dollar to the Australian government after the Crown declined to renew the hundred-year lease. The government gave the land back to the Aboriginals, who never raised another cow or grew another chicken, hog, or vegetable. The government fed them and gave them a weekly check for booze. The only thing Allan got out of the deal was his Australian stock saddle, which he had used to run brumbies around Battle Creek. He would later learn that

CHAPTER FOUR

In the beginning. The dawn of time for the early ancestors of modern man, seven million years ago. The DNA of Sahelanthropus and Orrorin was already millions of years old, pumping in the blood of primates. These creatures of the Miocene Epoch lived in trees to escape animals larger than themselves. Four million years ago, they came to ground. It took another million years for them to walk short distances crouched over. They communicated in grunts and gestures. A million years later, preman was making tools to scratch roots from the earth, and he fashioned weapons to kill creatures smaller than himself. He was growing teeth to rip flesh off bone, ingesting protein, building muscle, and thus gaining power over even larger beasts. The brain of the hominids, the prehuman species, was small and seated deep, back and low in the skull. It processed information of sight, hearing, and smell – and executed quick, evasive response to danger. Finally, man discovered fire, making it easier for him to consume more meat, the cooking process delivering digestibility. Thus he grew rapidly in sizes and strength.

When preman met his first horse, the animal stood about as tall as man's waist. Since the beginning, he was on man's food chain. But each had a brain identical in size, each producing electromagnetic energy that placed man and beast on the same electrical grid. The horse brain processed survival information. The horse would never develop tools, never open new lines of communication. His brain would develop in mass very little, because there was no need. Instead, the horse would evolve to have greater speed, relying exclusively on its original monolith brain.

Thus, preman and horse spoke the same "language" in man's dawn of evolution. The horse had already been in existence 55 million years in some form or another. Man and horse communication initially was based on sounds and posture, but soon morphed into a direct line from man-brain to horse-brain, with sounds and gestures becoming less important as communication was repeated constantly and each could "see" what the other was thinking, their electrical energy being compatible. They developed an ability to transmit pictures, their brain cells, at this stage of evolution, in perfect tune.

Over millions of years, this communication between man and horse would diminish. Fossils found in Africa date modern man at 200,000 years ago, and evidence showed his frontal lobe and neocortex were developing to handle language and a growing intelligence. New layers of brain covered the original old brain identical to the brain of the horse. This change, however, did not happen to everybody leading into modern times. Some very special people would miss the frontal lobe evolution. They would keep their ability to communicate with animals in the old way, emitting an electromagnetic energy that creatures lower on the animal scale were extremely sensitive to. But these people in modern times would be challenged in communicating with modern man, whose brain evolved with totally different wiring. Twentieth-century science would eventually call these people *autistic*.

CHAPTER FIVE

Saturday, January 23. Emma and her mother are in the kitchen, a slow day on the ranch.

"Mom, I go Suzanne's. We ride."

"Fine with me. They got mostly mules over there. Is there a horse you can ride?"

"Yeah, horses. But I ride mules okay."

Millie nods, and then, as if on an afterthought, says, "Do you know Jules is home?"

"Yes," says Emma, trying to sound casual.

Suzanne's place is a mile south on North Kanan Dume Road. Suzanne is in the same grade as Emma. Suzanne is Emma's closest girlfriend and has always known Emma was "different."

Millie drives Emma to Suzanne's place. When they arrive, Suzanne's mother, Barbara, walks down the driveway of her home, Suzanne at her side.

"Okay, you know where the tack is," says Barbara. "Suzanne, saddle mules today. Rocket and Sundance. They need work."

"Yes, Mother."

The girls saddle up with special mule saddles, built on bars straighter than would work on horses. They are Western saddles, but Emma has no problem with the change of equipment. She rides any saddle. Mostly, she is concerned with the comfort of the horse or, in this case, mule. They brush, saddle, fit cruppers around tails, and set off, up toward the Backbone Trail, Emma's regular route.

It is a beautiful midwinter afternoon in the Santa Monica Mountains. Creeks are flowing, purple sage coming in, filling the air with fragrance, spider fern spreading. The hills are splashed with yellow from mustard grass. The ground is still soft. The mules move effortlessly across the ruts.

Emma has ridden with Suzanne many times. She is no stranger to mules. She does not see them as so different from horses, except, perhaps, they demand more gentle treatment. There is a story Emma's dad told her that she would never forget. He said, "If you put a horse in a trailer and you go down the road and you have a crash, it is a terrible drama to remove the horse from the crashed trailer, and it will take a great deal of retraining to get the horse back in the trailer. Now, put a mule in a trailer and go down the road and have a crash, the mule will never forget that *you* put him in the trailer."

Emma is on Rocket, Suzanne on Sundance. The mules are about equal height, 15.1 hands, 900 pounds. The girls move out and ride on up the trail. They talk about school, friends, life at home. They ride together regularly. They talk on cell phones, text and Twitter, and know each other intimately. What Emma likes about Suzanne is that she never makes her feel uncomfortable though sometimes her words are not right or she repeats herself or her tone is not exactly correct. With Suzanne, Emma can speak freely.

The girls ride off, heading into the hills, the afternoon sun dipping on their left, crickets and insects playing their tunes.

* * *

Millie and Barbara are in the spacious kitchen of Barbara's ranch-style home.

"So … Jules is back home," Millie offers.

"Yes, he is," confirms Barbara.

"Emma knows," Millie says. "They hung out a lot as kids – remember? – always messing with horses. Never had to worry much about them."

"Something to drink," asks Barbara, "tea, coffee, wine …?"

"Make that wine! I need a drink. Wish I didn't!"

"How so?" Barbara asks, setting two glasses. The Saddle Rock chardonnay is chilled.

"Farm's not going well."

"Oh, everybody's in that boat today."

Millie lifts her glass and in that moment looks out the kitchen window at a man splitting logs. The man is brown-skinned, with long black hair tied back in a ponytail. He is swinging an axe with forceful, sure cuts. Millie cannot help but notice his muscles, his back rippling and mirrored with sweat. He is also strikingly handsome. Somewhere deep in her consciousness, warnings sound, loud and clear. So this is the boy who always fascinated Emma when they were kids. What will she think now?

"Is that Jules?" Millie ventures.

Barbara sighs. "That's Jules all right."

Millie looks incredulous. "Wow, he's sure all grown-up!"

"Seven years, he's been gone. You'll remember we sent him back to Ohio to live with Zac, his biological dad, but that was a mistake. I thought Zac had changed. I was wrong. We visited Jules in Columbus as much as we could, and he seemed happy, but his grades were never good. And then ... there were his legal problems ..."

"Yeah," says Millie, "you and I have agonized about that from time to time."

Barbara sighs. "He didn't do it, you know. Jules beat that guy to a pulp because of what he was doing to that girl."

Then Barbara turns somber and says, "The prosecutors said Jules got into a jealous rage and went completely out of control before his last visit to Juvenile Hall. They said Jules had been stalking the girl. If you ask me, they came down on Jules because Jules is half black. They're racists. And I think they took out their feelings toward Zac, being black. They just figured any son of a con is a con, especially a black con."

"Yeah, wouldn't happen today with Obama as president."

"He was just flirting, as boys will," continues Barbara. "That's natural. Jules was attracted to the girl, and he was talking with her, and this other guy comes in and pushes him aside and grabs the girl by the arm to take her out of the room. Jules just couldn't stand seeing this thug push her around. Jules is not a hothead, but he will make a decision and act quickly. He thought what he was doing was right, though he should have eased off after he made his point. He just kept pummeling the guy."

Together the women watch the axe moving up and down as if attached to a machine, wood chips flying, great hunks of timber falling like wedges of cake. Jules is in a tank top, sweat-glistened arms rippled with muscle.

Millie says, "You know, Emma missed Jules a lot when he left way back when. She doesn't show emotion, as you know, that being part of her condition, but I knew she missed him. He would tell her all those horse stories, always had some history book with him. She loved it, because Emma has always had this really strange thing for horses. It's like she was born in another time, and then somehow transported here, to modern times."

"Yeah," says Barbara," Jules was – is – lost in history. He kind of hides in his books. He has his own private world, like Emma has her own world. But we didn't worry. We thought that maybe one day Jules would be a history major or something. Trouble is, all he did was read those old books, babbling on about Alexander the Great, Attila the Hun, Genghis Khan, you name it. He was never, ever like other boys. He was – still is – obsessed with the old world, which he adopted as *his* world."

The women look out the window in silence, and Millie appraises Jules and realizes there is a quality of distinct beauty about the way he moves, the way he looks. A beauty, she knows, most young women would find hard to resist. "They sure fed him well in Juvenile Hall," Millie says.

Barbara laughs. "Oh yeah, they did that. They also turned him into a wrestler. He was easily the best among 150 young men. Never lost. Pumped iron and read books."

"Yeah, I heard that too. Heard he nearly killed somebody in Juvie, and they wouldn't let him fight anymore."

"That part's true," says Barbara. "And this confused Jules. He could not understand why they trained him to hurt people, and then when he did just that, they banned him from wrestling. Broke his heart, it did."

"Doesn't seem right," consoles Millie.

"So we worry about him," continues Barbara. "He's so angry, like he doesn't fit in. We're kind of afraid to let him out of our sight. What saved him in Juvenile Hall was that we were allowed to give him as many books as he wanted. He reads and gets into his own world, mentally locked away so he doesn't have to talk to anybody. Like other kids do with those video games."

"Well, isn't that a good thing, like a constant ongoing education?" Millie ventures.

"If it keeps him out of trouble, I'll be happy. What I'm really pleased about is he's been accepted for a job at the Thousand Oaks City Library," Barbara replies.

"Wow, that's great!"

"Yeah, he'll love that, up to his armpits in books! Next year, we're going to look at Community College for him."

Millie nods. "That would be wonderful. He'll find his way. Emma loves to read too, probably for the same reason. Slips into her own world. Loves anything with vampires. Loves all that strange Gothic stuff. I'm just terrified she's gonna ask me if she can get a tattoo or put a ring in her lip or someplace else. I try to read that stuff, and it puts me to sleep. Reads like a foreign language."

Outside, Jules buries the axe in a stump, positions the wheelbarrow, and starts loading.

"He's grown into a handsome young man," Millie observes. "Doesn't look like a reader. Looks more like one of those warrior savages in the books he reads."

Barbara chuckles. "Yeah, got the looks from his father's side. Zac didn't read, though. About all he knew to do with a book was use it to level furniture. That and as a missile. He threw books at me all the time."

"You read a lot?"

"True. Got Jules started when he was very young."

"Where's Zac now?"

"Still in Ohio, I suspect. Heard he beat up his new wife – again – so he's probably back in prison. Anyhow, it's what Jules wanted, really wanted, to move back in with Zac after his last visit to Juvenile Hall. I made a mistake, letting Jules go back there, but I was convinced Zac had changed. My instincts told me not to let him go back to his real dad, but I let it happen anyhow. I guess I wanted him to make his own assessment of his biological father. Rob didn't want him to go back either. Rob has always been wonderful with Jules, treats him like his own son, always has. Rob is a good man, and I am very lucky I met him and that he asked me to marry him. So now Jules is back home here, and we're really happy about that! But … sometimes I ask myself, is this all there is? I wonder if I've ever been in love, really. And then my imagination wanders … What's that they say about grass being greener on the other side?"

Silence falls between the two women as they watch Jules move off with the wheelbarrow, out of view.

"Ah, that's normal," offers Millie. "I feel that about every second day. I read a romance novel and take a big sigh, and life goes on."

The two sip wine and keep looking out the window, although Jules has long disappeared.

"So," says Barbara, after a while, "how is *your* girl?"

"Oh, Emma, she has her problems," says Millie, "not with us, but with her friends. They're so cruel. It's that catty age. The girls are all so competitive. And I'm worried some boy is going to take advantage of her, you know."

Barbara contemplates her wine. "Yeah, I know. Emma's growing into a head-turner. Drop-dead gorgeous!"

Then Millie asks, "Did you ever wish you had married Zac?"

Barbara is caught off guard by the change of subject. Then: "It was all too complicated. I left him, and then soon after, I found I was pregnant by Zac with Jules. I called him, and he said he would do the best he could to help me. Then he got in with a bad crowd and ended up in jail. So, I raised Jules on my own for a year, and then I met Rob. Right off, got pregnant with Suzanne. Overly fertile, I guess!"

Barbara looks out the window, as if to find the answers written there. And then she admits, "I never got over Zac. I know you'll think I'm crazy, but sometimes I think I am still in love with him. I think of him all the time, to be honest. He was my first true love. And then I met Rob. Rob was always great with Jules, and with me. He never interfered with my relationship with Zac and Jules.

I don't really deserve Rob, and I feel guilty still thinking about Zac the way I do, about the way we made love. I should be happy but … I just don't know. I always tried so hard to make Zac part of Jules's life. I shouldn't have. It was a mistake."

More silence. Barbara chuckles. "You know, sometimes I think there are problems with Jules, not autistic problems like Emma has. He speaks more or less normally, but his mind drifts off … like he's someplace else. His grades were barely passable when he was in school. The teachers said if it was not for his grasp of the English language, he would have had no grades. He writes so well he makes wrong answers read brilliantly. But he has no energy to write. He just … reads."

"Maybe," offers Millie, "maybe he's got ADD. He never seemed autistic to me – just … different. Closed up like a clam when he met people, including me. Does he still do that?"

"Oh, yes. I remember you telling me about Emma, how she knows what her horse thinks, how she 'talks' with animals on this strange level but has trouble talking with people. Well, Jules is a little like that. Now, mind you, I have never caught him actually having conversations with horses, but he does seem to be in contact with them somehow. He never has to halter horses. They just … follow him. He looks in a direction, and they go to where he's looking. He's always done that. And now that he's back home, he's doing it again. Do you think that's strange?"

Millie smiles. "I know somebody else who does that, and a whole lot more."

"Not to pry here," ventures Barbara, "but I remember you telling me about that affair, back when you and Allan were having problems. Now Harry, *he* sure was good looking! Did you ever wish you had married him instead of Allan?"

"Oh, yes! Many times. But Allan loves me and takes care of me, and I just couldn't leave him for what I called my Studly! Allan loves and cares for Emma too … although he doesn't understand her as I do. He gets impatient, frustrated."

"Where's Studly now?" Barbara asks.

"Back in London, I think. Haven't heard from him for years, which is just as well. I don't think I could trust myself."

"Then we're both in the same boat," ventures Millie. "Both desperate housewives!"

And the room echoes their laughter.

* * *

Out on the trail, Emma is receiving pictures from Rocket, nothing special, just … this is okay, nice to be out. The communication from mule to her is no different than it has always been with Tower. Mules, she decides, just seem more sensitive, temperamental.

The girls ride over the knoll, down a deep ravine, and thread up a narrow trail on the other side, with the sun on the left dropping so low it finally slides below the crest of the mountain range. They are in the moon's half-light.

Suddenly Suzanne's mule stops, front legs parted and planted firmly. Sundance drops his head, snorts, turns, and runs, retreating. Rocket also freezes. Emma feels his fear, and then sees the picture Rocket sees. A mountain cub is off in the bushes, ten yards to the left. Emma looks around for the mother, and the answer comes from Rocket. He lifts his head, pointing with his long ears, and there, perched on a rock twenty feet above is the mother, about 250 pounds. Rocket turns, as if to bolt, but Emma pats his neck. She keeps tension on both reins, just light enough so Rocket can feel the contact. Then she asks him to back away, keeping his face to the lioness. The big cat crouches now, as if to spring, and the message from Rocket to Emma is, "Let's get the hell out of here! Now!" But Emma's message to Rocket is, "We're okay. Just keep backing away, facing the lioness, and the threat to her cub will lessen. The lioness just wants to protect her baby. So, don't turn your back on her!"

Slowly, Emma and Rocket back down the trail, and the field of tension eases. When it is safe to turn around, Emma does so, and a hundred yards down the hill, she catches up with Suzanne, who had been watching, frozen in fear.

"What happened?" Suzanne blurts out. "Why did you stay there? Weren't you scared?"

"Yes," says Emma, "but more scary for mother lion. Worried for baby."

Suzanne looks at Emma and frowns. "You're crazy. That cat was going to kill us!"

"No. Just wanted us gone."

"She … looked like she was going to attack. I was scared. Weren't you scared?"

"Yes, me afraid. But mother lion speak to me."

"So, now you're talking to mountain lions!"

Emma gives Suzanne a puzzled look.

"Emma, you *are* crazy."

"Me no crazy," says Emma quietly, almost to herself.

"Okay, you're not crazy. You're … just not like anybody else."

"Yes."

The girls ride along in silence.

"I just see pictures," says Emma.

"Yeah, yeah," says Suzanne, rolling her eyes. She has heard all this before. Then she asks, "Should we tell … about what happened tonight?"

"No. Bad idea. Mother call police. Park rangers come with guns."

"You're right."

Again, a conspiratorial silence. The balmy night embraces all living creatures. Somewhere a coyote yips. Two others chorus. There is a pack. Some small fuzzy animal is about to die.

* * *

Back home now, Emma has fed the horses, has eaten dinner, and is spread facedown on her bed. The room is dark, and she feels a heavy tiredness. She drifts off and is overcome by that familiar feeling. She wants to go there. Now!

Suddenly her world is clear. She is galloping on a horse, along a wide, slow-flowing river, where a dawn mist is rising, but she is not in charge of the horse. In fact, she is tied to the horse, arms forward, wrists bound under the neck of the horse. Her ankles are lashed under the belly of the horse. She looks up and sees a man with a leopard-skin head cover, the skin trailing down his bare back. She has seen this man before. And then she remembers, and her stomach runs cold. It is hard to hold up her head, so she lets it fall. Ground passes beneath her at great speed. She wants to scream, but her breath is short. Now, turning away from the river, up a steep bank and onto flat ground. Emma hears voices, many voices. She tilts her head and sees tents, fires, many men, all carrying swords and weapons. No women, no children. Dogs yelp, and somewhere horses neigh. She is in what looks like a warriors' camp. Now the horse stops, and moments later, she feels her ties being cut, and she is pulled off the horse. She drops to the ground. Every bone in her body aches.

"Attila, I bring you this piece of live animal that the green-eyed one let live in the raid of yesterday. I was ready to slaughter her like a pig, but he stopped me."

"Why did you bring her here?" Attila demands.

"So that I could kill her in your presence – and avenge the life taken by the green-eyed one, who killed the warrior Aka while he was trying to deliver this wretch to her death."

Emma looks up now, and into the face of the man being called Attila. He has olive skin and high cheekbones, eyes piercing and brown and strangely slit.

Attila turns slightly, without taking his eyes off Emma, still sitting on the ground, her legs and feet bare under the deerskin covers. She was wearing this when the savages attacked her village, and the man with green eyes saved her. She closes her eyes and in her mind again feels the warm blood spurting on her as the man with the green eyes sliced the throat of her attacker.

Attila barks in disgust, "Bring me this man who killed Aka to save this female animal!"

Warriors gather. There is much shouting. Emma sees a figure coming through the crowd, parting them as he moves toward Attila. It is him. The man with the green eyes, and ponytail in braided leather. This is the one who saved her from Leopard Man. His sword is at his side.

Attila regards him for several moments, eyes narrowing. He spits words: "So, it is you, Zehun. One of my strongest. Why ... why did you kill a warrior to save this worthless creature?"

"She was unarmed. She posed no danger," says Zehun.

Attila cocks his head, momentarily puzzled. "Ah, deer and hogs pose no danger and they're not armed, but we kill them all the time. So, why is this creature different?"

"She is not a deer. She is a Hun."

Attila sighs, frustrated, always a sign of danger for anybody within sword reach. "She is not *a Hun! She is not one of us. She is worthless. Anybody who is not a Hun is worthless!"*

Leopard Man breaks the moment and moves forward, sword drawn. "Let me kill her now, and take revenge for Aka!"

Attila shoots him a hard glance and then snaps, "She did not kill Aka!" Attila then pulls his own sword, causing the growing circle of warriors to gasp collectively and step back. Almost always when Attila does this, somebody dies. Then Attila points the sword at the green-eyed warrior and says, "Zehun, he killed Aka – so first he *must die!"*

Leopard Man steps forward, sword raised, and screams, "So I will first kill him, and then kill her!"

Attila lowers his sword and now, for the first time, looks around the crowd. He is center stage among his fighting warriors. He is amused at all the possibilities this presents. "Okay. You can kill her, but first ..." He turns to the crowd, his demeanor demanding, milking attention. He continues, "... but first you must step over the dead body of Zehun to kill her." This statement is greeted with loud cheers. "But if he kills you, *he has the right to do what he wishes with this worthless creature," Attila says, kicking dirt at Emma.*

Warriors chant. Feet stamp. Dust rises.

Immediately, the two men pull swords and circle each other. Leopard Man is first to move, coming forward with heavy short swings, forcing Zehun back, struggling suddenly to regain his footing. He had not expected such a rush. Zehun ducks as Leopard Man swings for what he feels will be the killer blow. The sword goes over Zehun's head, and for an instant Leopard Man has his left side exposed to Zehun, who moves forward and in a flash swings up with his own sword and catches the hilt of Leopard Man's sword, and twists savagely. Zehun has disarmed Leopard Man in exactly the same way as he did yesterday. Leopard Man screams with rage as he stumbles back, falls, and Zehun holds his sword at his throat. Without taking his eyes off his opponent, Zehun addresses Attila, "He is not worthy of my sword. He is a good warrior for you, so I let him live. You will need him to kill Romans."

"Your call," barks Attila, a little bored now.

Zehun steps back and turns now to Emma. He is looking at her and marveling at how beautiful she is, in a strange, exotic way. He has never quite seen such beauty, such blonde hair brushing her face. He is puzzled now, as her face crunches into horror and the air fills with her screams. He realizes she is looking past him, and he turns as Leopard Man is almost upon him, sword raised to strike. There is fire and hatred in his eyes. The sword comes down, but Zehun drops to earth and rolls to the side, simultaneously holding up his sword right under where Leopard Man has thrown himself for what he was sure would be a killer blow. Leopard Man falls squarely on Zehun's blade with all his weight. A bloody length of steel protrudes from his back, and blood chokes off a scream, replacing it with the eerie gurgling of death.

A thunderous cheer from the crowd, so loud Emma's ears hurt, and then the noise drifts away and a black silence moves in. The next sound Emma hears is of her own steady breathing as she lies in her bed, safe at home in Malibu. She is still facedown and fully clothed. Her heart is pounding so fast she can feel it beating against her chest. And soon, she is in a deep sleep of another kind, where there is no light, no sound. Only a soft, evolving peace.

CHAPTER SIX

Friday, February 5, 5:00 p.m. The Armbrust farm. Emma is saddling Tower. She is happy, at week's end. Tower is anxious to be up in the mountains. Horse and girl exchange pictures while she adjusts the saddle blanket and secures the girth. The other horses have been annoying Tower, and Manuel has been pushing him around, once smacking him on the rump with a mucking shovel. Emma sees herself riding with the setting sun at her back, enjoying the early evening coming up from the ocean 1,500 feet below on Pacific Coast Highway. Tower gives a deep, noisy exhale. He is also happy with that picture.

Soon they are cantering along the fire trail. The air is clear and crisp. Emma is glad she has her oilskin riding coat. Always, when she is on Tower, she thinks life is perfect. Nothing makes her happier than the smell of his sweat, his warmth between her legs. Up ahead now, Emma sees a person in red shorts and loose white T-shirt. The figure is running, strides powerful and even, black hair in a ponytail. At first Emma thinks it is a woman, because of the ponytail, but from a hundred yards she sees it is not. The back is too broad, the legs too muscled. Now almost upon the figure, she slows to a walk, and then her heart stops and her eyes lock on the leather thong tying back his hair. She has seen this before. She halts Tower. The man stops too, his breathing heavy, but even. Tower's ears shoot forward, and he lowers his head, gazing intently at the man. The recognition is instant for Tower. Before the man turns, Emma knows it's him. This is confirmed by Tower's transmitting images. It is the man she has seen many, many times in her dreams – the man who rescued her with his sword when the savages attacked her village in the vision she saw just days ago. This is the man who fought for her life in front of Attila, the man who killed the savage with the leopard-skin head cover. But how could this be? That was a vision. This is reality. The effect on her is physical – dizzying, deep, and scary. This is someone she has known before. This is somebody who has a very important connection to her – why, why?

The young man has turned, and Emma feels her mouth drop. Her throat is suddenly dry. The man smiles, the fading light catching the deep green of his eyes. He is about her age, she reckons. She is speechless, both because he looks so familiar and because she has never, ever seen a more handsome man. Has she seen him in a movie? *No* – she has seen him in her visions, but now here she is looking at him for real, and he is even more handsome than how she sees him in her visions. Emma feels he recognizes her too. Emma is the first to speak. "I know you …"

"Yes, you do. I'm Jules. You were at the house last week, to go riding with Suzanne and the mules. I saw you, but … I stayed out of sight."

"Why did you not come up to me?"

"I wasn't ready. We were together long ago," he says. "We were just kids."

"Yes."

"I used to read you stories from my horse history books …"

Emma frowns.

41

"Well, let's start over. I'm Jules, Suzanne's brother." He laughs and adds, "Tower recognizes me, at least!"

Emma receives an image from Tower. Jules is much younger in this image. His hair is short, and he is quite thin, not heavily muscled like he is now. She recognizes the barn at Suzanne's place. She is confused and more than a little troubled that the man Zehun, who has appeared in her vision, looks just like Jules.

Jules is at her side now, extending up his hand. Emma reaches out uncertainly. The man's grip is warm and firm. His eyes seem to devour her whole being. She hears him talking. "I must say, you have grown into a beautiful woman. You are the same, but … so beautiful."

There is a strained moment, and then Jules adds quickly, "The way you get around the mountains is much easier than how I do it. But I love to run. I like to feel my heart pound."

If only he knew, she thinks. She is aware of a rising heat in her cheeks, and desperately hopes it does not show.

Emma realizes she hasn't let his hand go, and now she does so with some urgency, suddenly remembering how she *hates* to touch people, or be touched. She feels her cheeks growing even hotter and wonders, *now he can surely see this!*

Jules looks into Emma's eyes, and she feels like he is examining every cell of her body. After a while, he says, "I remember you – but I never remember you were so … like a picture on the cover of a fashion magazine!"

Emma feels her words stumble. "Thank … you."

Jules laughs and steps back. "I remember the stories you loved the most were about Attila and how he conquered the world and wanted to marry the beautiful sister of the governor of Constantinople."

"I remember," says Emma. "You told about people first ride horses. Women warriors."

Jules shakes his head. "Wow, that's a memory!"

"I see them," she says, tapping her helmet.

"Hey," says Jules, suddenly inspired, "why don't we meet here tomorrow, same time, and we'll pull up a rock someplace, and I'll read that history to you again. Let's pick up where we left off, years ago."

"Yes … yes," she hears herself say.

"Well, gotta go. Three more miles will make my ten!"

And then he is gone, running through the trees with the ease and grace of a deer.

Emma watches him until trees paint over him. Now it is clear. She remembers more and more of the time she spent with Jules back when they were not yet teens. She remembers how clever he seemed, and how much emotion he put into telling her stories about the horse, and about Alexander the Great and Attila and Genghis Khan. They would sit in the tack room or up in the hayloft or on the bench overlooking the corral. They sat under the big coral tree in front of the barn at Suzanne's house, or on the rock down by the stream that ran behind the barn after the rains. Whenever anybody approached, he would shut his book and not talk. He told her many times he knew other people thought he was "weird," but he didn't care. She told him people thought she was "weird" too. They would laugh.

Images rushed back now, a flood. Emma is no longer confused. Jules had left her life when he was taken away years ago, back to Ohio, but he remained in her soul. Now he is back – for real. But this does not answer the big question: Why does he look exactly like Zehun, who is in another time and in a strange place, far, far away?

CHAPTER SEVEN

Monday, February 8, late afternoon. Emma rides Tower out of the farm, across Kanan Road, and heads off into the hills. She had slept fleetingly last night. She questions why she is doing this, but there is nothing she can do about it. She is drawn to Jules by some incredible power.

She rounds a bend in the trail, and there is Jules, in his running shorts, with a bag slung over his muscled shoulder. He grins broadly. "So you didn't stand me up after all!"

Emma smiles.

They lock eyes, then Jules says, "Well, I have a book here with the part of the history you used to like. But I'd get a stiff neck reading to you while you're sitting up there."

Emma climbs off Tower, and she stands in front of Jules. She is amazed at how she has to look up to make eye contact.

"Come," says Jules, "there is some nice shade over there. Let's sit a while."

They settle under a huge oak tree. Emma has tied Tower to a tree. From his bag Jules pulls out a heavy book.

"I read this to you years ago, and it is where it all began for man and the horse. It's about the Sarmatians, the first to ride horses, and they included the first women warriors, five thousand years ago. But first, I'll read to you where the horse came from."

And so Jules opens *The Noble Horse* by Monique and Hans D. Dossenbach, finds a page he has marked, and begins to read, paraphrasing where necessary.

Fifty-five million years ago, there was Hyracotherium (Eohippus), small, timid, about the size of a small dog, standing ten to seventeen inches. Four legs, feet multitoed, four on each front, three on each hind. Walked with head level, a long, solid tail. Inhabited hot, damp jungles, fed on leaves of low cypress limbs. Remains of this horse have been found in Europe, the Wind River basin in Wyoming, and the Wasatch Range in Utah. Every 5 million years, the horse gained half its size.

Enter Oligocene Epoch 37 million years ago, migrating across a land bridge between North America and Europe. This horse (Mesohippus) adapted to changes in climate, in a temperate world where deciduous trees were outnumbered by conifers. He no longer needed webbed toes to stop sinking in mud, so he grew a hoof, which gave him greater speed over grasslands. The stump of his tail grew shorter, more bushy.

Merychippus appeared 17 million years ago, and for the first time resembled today's horse. He grew teeth to rip and grind grasses. Hooves thickened and hardened, but he was still only thirty-six inches tall. By the time this creature had morphed into Pliohippus, migrations were happening all over the planet. This evolution spun off numerous relatives: tarpan, zebra, and wild ass. The steppes of Russia cradled the first distinctive relatives of today's horse, and over millions of years they migrated west and south, with new breeds evolving whenever a herd settled.

Preman and horse coexisted for millions of years with a relationship where man was the hunter, the horse prey.

"You mean we *ate* them?" Emma asks, incredulous.

"Yes, but listen. There's more. Now don't interrupt me!"

And Jules continues in a tone that fascinates Emma:

The horse evolved in many different physical varieties, but with very little cerebral change. Evolving horses didn't need to get smarter, just faster. Man, concurrently, was evolving greatly in both his brain and his physical appearance. He grew smarter, outthinking what he couldn't outrun. Man changed greatly; horse did not. Then, an acceleration of change occurred around 30,000 BC, and man was becoming more civilized. He strived to make life easier. Early man began domesticating horses, to avoid having to hunt them. They milked mares, ripped off hides, ate the meat. Great herds were appearing on the steppes north of the Black Sea. The Mongols evolved with the horse at a pace faster than other evolving cultures. They believed in the Centaur – a creature half man, half horse. In Mesopotamia, by the fourth millennium BC, oxen were being harnessed, along with onagers and the wild ass of Central Asia. By the third millennium BC, a nose ring appeared for steering and control. These yoked animals pulled plows and sleds, and then soon after, these vehicles rolled on crude wheels. Early man put the cart before the horse. The wheel was evolving. By the second millennium BC, chariots were being used by hunters in Syria. The first bridle appeared, with cheek pieces made of bone, and bits from sinew and rope.

Emma moves closer to Jules as he reads. She is so close she can feel his body heat. She is looking down at the page as if she is reading it too. She is not, of course. She knows she cannot read that fast.

Jules continues:

> The earliest people to use horses for war were the Sarmatians, whose homeland was between the Black and Caspian seas, in what is now southern Russia. They were a mixture of Greek and Iranian. Their recorded history goes back to 6,000 BC. They galloped into the third century BC with man's first primitive wood-frame saddle, a construction that was prompted by this tribe's use of heavy cavalry. They wore armor and used a very heavy lance, something the Greeks called a "barge pole." They were without doubt the first mounted warriors to charge into an enemy formation in a style that would continue in cavalry for thousands of years. They needed a saddle with a high back and front, so they could keep seated while driving their lance into enemy who, in the beginning, were not mounted. The Sarmatians were extremely violent. They killed for the joy of killing, and the plunder and party atmosphere it provided. They carried scalps and ears and other body parts of their slain enemies as trophies on their saddles and bridles. Strangely, four thousand years later, Native Americans would do the same. The connection has never been explained.

"That's disgusting," Emma gasps.

Jules sighs, exasperated. "Please, no more interruptions!"

Emma looks away from the book, lowering her head apologetically.

Jules continues:

The Sarmatians were also the first to use women as warriors. Archaeological sites in Southern Ukraine revealed that about 20 percent of warrior graves located in the lower Don and lower Volga contained females dressed for battle as if they were men. Scholars believe this promoted the Greek myth of the Amazons. These women were feared for their courage and extreme brutality. They castrated the enemy, dried the testicles, then threaded the "nuts" with a leather thong hung from a loop over their ears. The longer the "earrings," the greater the status of the female warrior. They killed the weakest male enemy and spared the strongest. These they hauled home to be used as breeding stock in special compounds. The women never married. When they became pregnant, they were retired from battle until the child was born. If it was a boy in good physical condition, he was saved, to be added to the breeding pool. Weak male babies were discarded. All girls were saved, to be trained as warriors, their rearing left to elders.

While the Sarmatians had primitive saddlery, there is no evidence they had a stirrup. That would come three thousand years later with Attila the Hun, who would use it as a tipping point of power against the Romans. He would also greatly improve the saddle created by the Sarmatians. Several hundred years before Attila – possibly as early as 500 BC – a "toe stirrup" was in use by East Indian cavalry. The big toe was inserted into a leather loop hung from each side of the saddle. Not surprisingly, the idea did not fly on the steppes of Southern Russia, where naked flesh froze in winter. A metal stirrup appeared in China around 400 BC, but it came only as one, not a pair, and was used as a mounting aid.

Emma looks at Jules in awe, is about to say something, but remains silent.

Jules catches this reaction. He smiles and continues reading:

> Meanwhile, some 10,500 years ago now, the genus *Equus* was migrating from its homeland in North America to the Old World, crossing the Bering land bridge that once connected Alaska and Siberia. While these horses spread out over Europe, Asia, and Africa, their relatives remaining in North America disappeared, reasons unknown. During the Ice Age, a primitive pony thrived in glacial landscapes. In European forests, the tarpan put its stamp on evolving warm-blooded horses. In Africa, a tall, long-legged horse was taking shape, while in the deserts of Asia, the fine-boned Arabian was emerging. While man continued to eat horses, cave paintings found in Lascaux and Pech Merle in France, and others in Altamira, Spain, revealed a growing mythical reverence for this animal. Man was impressed with the speed of the horse and how, seemingly, it could outrun most other creatures. This became the horse's salvation, as it grew no teeth for ripping flesh, and instead developed very efficient molars to grind grasses …

It is almost dark now. The sun has dropped over the rim of the Santa Monica Mountains, and a golden backlight blazes the ridgetop.

Jules closes the book, and Emma is staring at him. She is speechless.

"Come on," says Jules with some urgency. "I didn't realize so much time has passed. Better get on Tower and head home!"

Emma looks alarmed. "Yes!"

"You'll be okay," says Jules in his most assuring voice.

"And you?"

Jules smiles. "I got here on two legs. I'll leave on two legs!"

Emma climbs up on Tower, gathers the reins, and then looks down at Jules. "Thank you. Love Sarmatian women – amazing."

And then she is gone, cantering off toward a rising moon.

CHAPTER EIGHT

Friday, February 26. Emma is happy school is over for the week. Her grades are okay, but she grows anxious about the distractions, the taunts. She is reluctant to bring this to the attention of her teachers because she knows they'll talk with her mother and then it would be a big discussion at home about her "special problems." Emma fears her parents are thinking of sending her to another doctor. She wants nothing more to do with doctors. She knows they can't "help," because she knows she does not need help. This is who she *is*. She is happy with that. It is the people around her who are strange. It is like they are unhappy because she is happy. From her viewpoint, most of the adults around her are not as happy as she is!

Emma is in her room now. She checks the lock. Her parents are watching television. She pulls open the lowest drawer of her dresser and, under a false bottom, finds lithographs she has stashed away. She spreads them on the bed. First is from Guizot's *L'Histoire de France*, 1870. It shows the Huns galloping on wild-eyed horses, muscled arms thrusting spears, spiked clubs and axes swinging from saddles, along with severed heads. The hooves of the front horse are about to trample a naked lady, whose bound hands are trying to reach for her baby. This picture has played over and over in Emma's mind; it's like she is *there*. She sees the blood – smells it!

In the next lithograph, Cimbric women are fighting the Romans at the end of the second century. Horses are falling and screaming, daggers and spears slicing flesh. Emma is *there*.

She wonders if this is what the Sarmatian women looked like, six hundred years before.

Next: Attila, shown in an Italian woodcut, where the artist was obviously convinced he was crossed with a hound. He gave Attila long pointed ears and a doglike snout. Emma knows there was no hound involved. But there was a horse involved. Yes, she decides, she could see Attila as part horse. She closes her eyes and visualizes Attila as she saw him the first time, when Zehun saved her, once again, from Leopard Man. Attila looked nothing like this woodcut.

There are other pictures of horses and weapons and battle scenes from *the Dark Ages*. They are shadowy and cruel, yet somehow beautiful. She wonders why she must hide these pictures, why she should not let her mother know. But this, she decides, must always be her secret, her private world. When she looks at these images, she can hear voices, hear the pounding of hooves, hear the clash of steel blades, hear the screams of the dying – can see the flow of blood. It is *real*. She is drawn to the images as delicately and as certainly as a light breeze ripples water on a pond. She closes her eyes now, and she knows she is going back there, this time willingly, almost eagerly. It is coming. She feels herself being carried, lifted, and now floating and speeding and twirling into a different but familiar place. She is so, so relaxed.

The mist clears and there he is, walking toward her, bloody sword in hand. Attila is laughing, and the warriors are still cheering. Beyond Zehun is the crumpled body of the savage with the leopard skin on his head. Blood is soaking through and flowing from the leopard skin. For a moment, it seems to Emma that there is a leopard that has been killed. She looks back up at Zehun, who is extending his left hand now. He pulls her to her feet. And holds up Emma's hand, as if to present her trophy-like to his fellow warriors. They roar approval. "You saved me," Emma says to Zehun.

Attila shakes his head, as if unable to comprehend the scene. "This man," he says to nobody in particular, "my warrior Zehun can have a thousand women, and he picks ... this." Attila curls his lip in disgust, and spits.

"Come," says Zehun, "I will take you back to your village." He barks an order, and two horses appear. He lifts her up on one horse as if she is a feather, springs onto his horse, and together, they head back off the plateau, down along the river.

"Thank you," she says. "And who ... who are you? And what am I doing in this place? And ... and ..." Emma stops mid-sentence as she listens to her own voice. She is speaking normally. No words in the wrong place, no flat tone.

"You know me. I am Zehun. I ride with Attila. I am his senior lieutenant. Now, let's go! You've seen me many times." He frowns and looks steadily at Emma now. "Are you ... all right?"

"Of course. I am all right! All right considering every time I see you, I am about to be killed," Emma says, marveling at how easy it is for her to speak in complete sentences when she is with Zehun.

Zehun laughs. "Ah, I see I anger you! You have spirit!"

Emma reins her horse around and rides off. Zehun catches up, and there is no more conversation. They ride for an hour, at a hand gallop, and then Zehun pulls to a stop. He is about to say something, but then Emma asks suddenly, "Why did you raid our village?"

Zehun thinks a minute and then says, "That's what we do; it's our life. We raid villages, so we can kill all the young men, so that when the Romans come, they will have nobody to enslave and train to kill us. For the same reason, we kill the cattle, so the Romans chasing us will have nothing to eat. Your village was not special."

"But ... but why?"

Zehun looks like he might ignore the question, but he shakes his head. He is clearly frustrated. "Look," he says, flatly, "Attila thinks it is better to kill males when they are young and defenseless, rather than when they are older and trained by the Romans. What part of that can you not understand?"

"Why ... then ... why did you save me?"

He looks at her and half smiles, green eyes sparkling like emeralds. "You don't look like the Romans would enslave you to fight." His eyes drop to her ankles, then continue up her body and lock in on her eyes. "But I am sure they would have other uses for you!"

They ride along in silence for five hours, and only once did Zehun stop, to make an observation. "You ride better than any female I have ever known. We Huns do not let our women ride with us when we're fighting. We could not stand the pain of knowing what the Romans would do with our women if they captured them."

"Riding is something I have always been able to do, because I love it."

"Who taught you?"

Emma is caught off guard with that question. Then she says: "I don't know. I've just always been able to ride. I love the way horses feel, how they think, even how they smell!" Again, she thinks to herself, how great it is being able to talk so freely, make complete sentences, and feel the other person is understanding everything. But while it is a relief, she ponders how it is strange because for her this perfect speech is not natural. It is like she is enjoying acting out another language; she is a great actress, and she is playing a role, speaking like this.

Then, after a while, Emma pulls her mind back to the reality of talking with Zehun. "So," she asks, "have ... you known many females?"

Now it is Zehun who is caught off guard. "What kind of question is that?"

"Well, I'd like to know!"

Zehun laughs. "I've known my share!" He spins the horse around and says: "Let's go!"

But Emma stays with a tight rein. "Hey," she says, "I'm not finished talking. I mean, have you ever felt special about another girl, you know ..."

Zehun turns, stops, takes a deep breath, and shakes his head. "You are a strange person. So many questions. I've never heard a woman talk to a man like this!"

"I can ask questions, can't I?"

"Okay, yes, you can." And then he looks at her for a long while and says: "I've never met another woman who has been as special to me as you are, if that is what you want to know."

"That's good," says Emma. And now it is she who wheels her horse and kicks his side. "I'm ready to go now!"

They gallop off together, threading through the timber. Emma is relishing the energy of her mount, and enjoying racing with Zehun now. He passes her. Then she passes him. And they are laughing as they race.

"You ride like a Hun warrior," says Zehun, grinning at her in admiration as they slow to a walk.

"Now that," says Emma, "was a blast.*"*

Zehun frowns. "A blast? What is a blast?"

Emma laughs. "I'll explain it to you sometime."

And they ride off at the walk, enjoying being close to each other, Emma feeling a tingle every time her knee brushes Zehun's leg.

Soon, they stop at the sight of campfires below. Emma recognizes her village.

"What is to happen with me?" Emma asks.

"I have plans for you."

"What plans?"

"We're going to be together forever. I have claimed you as my own."

Zehun turns his horse, not waiting for a comment. "I have Romans to kill," he calls over his shoulder.

"But ... wait," Emma calls after him.

Zehun stops, turns, comes back. "That's your village down there. You need to go back."

"I'm ... afraid. When will I see you again?"

Zehun shakes his head and dismounts. Emma does the same, and she stands in front of him.

"Do not be afraid. I am watching you, always."

They are standing so close Emma feels the warmth of his body; she smells his scent, mixed with horse sweat. Emma realizes he is holding her at arm's length, his massive hands on either side of her body. She is feeling great warmth coming from his presence, and she finds it strange that she loves being touched by this man. All her life she has been terrified of being touched, and now ... it is so ... different, so welcome.

Slowly, ever so slowly, Zehun pulls her to him, and she is cradled in the massive strength of his chest. Breathing is difficult. Her head is light. Butterflies invade her stomach. Her mouth is dry.

"I will let you go here," says Zehun, stepping back now. "Nobody in your village would welcome a Hun."

"I saw many men in the village killed. But my father, he escaped with my mother. I saw them leave."

"He would not have 'escaped,'" says Zehun. "They let him go. He is too old to kill. Who is caring for you?"

"I don't need anybody to care for me."

Zehun rolls his eyes. "I have not observed that! Every time I turn around, you need saving!"

Emma looks down, and then says, "You were there when I needed you, I admit."

Zehun pulls her closer to him, and she feels his cheek burning her face. "I have been assigned by the gods to take care of you."

Emma's breathing seems to stop as he presses his hard chest against her.

And they stand together like that for a very long time.

"When will I see you again?" Emma asks.

"Soon. We are pressing north now, to meet the Romans. They are circling."

"Will you be all right?"

He slaps the hilt of his sword. "Do not worry for me. Worry for the Romans! Death awaits them!"

For just a moment he looks as if he is turning to leave, but then he steps forward and holds Emma again. This time it is a very long embrace. Emma feels her body tremble, and then seem to crumble.

Zehun steps back, lifts her hand, and kisses it. "You are more beautiful than the most exquisite flower," he says, looking down at her, "with eyes more blue than the bluest sky, hair more golden than gold itself. You have been sent to me by the gods, and I swear to them I will take care of you, this treasure."

She is speechless.

Slowly he pulls her to him again, and she feels his mouth on her mouth, softly embracing her lips. Her whole body goes limp. She can barely stand.

And suddenly, almost savagely, he pulls her to him and she falls back, but his massive arms cradle her, and ever so gently she feels the ground. Now Zehun is beside her, his hands cupping her face, and now exploring her body, and she can't believe what is happening. There is a wetness she has never felt before, and now she wants him to continue, but she is at the same time terrified.

"My little angel, you radiant star, with skin as soft as driven snow ... you tremble!"

"I'm ... I'm maybe not ready."

"I kill with the savageness of a lion, but I make love as gently as wings give flight to a butterfly."

And he was right. This she discovers. Never had she known such a complete fullness, like a vessel that could hold no more. She is brimming over with happiness.

And then, in the mist and the beautiful forest, Emma experiences another sensation, a lasting and deep, penetrating warmth she had never before experienced.

Then Zehun is gone, galloping along the river, man and horse moving as one, until they are absorbed by the forest.

* * *

Emma is conscious now in her bedroom. She is looking at her hands. They are shaking. She is holding the lithographs. Quickly she places them back in her secret drawer, secures them away, and then climbs back into bed and studies the light in her mind growing dimmer and dimmer and then flickering toward blackness. Emma is exhausted. The images do that to her every time. She did not expect to "travel" like she did, right here, holding her treasures. But it happened. It was very, very pleasant, she concludes. She thinks of Jules now living here nearby in the hills of Malibu, and she thinks of Zehun, in another place long ago and far away, and is mystified by how she could visit them both. Yes, indeed, she decides, they *must* be the same person. She catches herself smiling. She feels her heart race at remembering her encounter with Jules on the trail. Sleep is a heavy black blanket gently pulling up from her feet. Emma's last thought is how very happy she is that Suzanne has been able to keep secret the incident with the mountain lioness. The last sensation before complete sleep is the scent of Zehun as he cradles her in his arms, and the feeling of his incredible power, yet with hands so gentle and soft – this mixed with the smell of burning wood carried in smoke curling up from a village in a place long ago and far away.

CHAPTER NINE

Saturday, March 27. A horse show at Trancas Riders and Ropers, overlooking the Pacific Ocean in Malibu. Emma is there with Tower, having trailered him down the hill with Suzanne's mule Sundance. There are thirty horses entered in her hunter/jumper class. It is a beautiful sunny day, a crisp breeze off the ocean, but still warm. Emma brushes Tower, saddles him, checks her own outfit, is unhappy with her hair, but shrugs as she buries it under a crash helmet. She is nervous. Jules is with his parents, up on the bleachers. How handsome he looks! In the past three weeks, they have met four times on the trail, the last two times at a waterfall, in an isolated area of the Santa Monica Mountains. Emma had known about this location for some time, and she was surprised to learn that Jules did not know about it. It was a secret she proudly shared. He was impressed. Each time they are together, Emma discovers something new about Jules, and about herself. She is drawn to him by a power she cannot explain nor understand. But she knows this power is a flame that warms her whole body. Emma tries to put Jules out of her mind now and think riding.

The first jumps are set at three feet. This eliminates half the class. Horses balk, run out, and rails fall. Tower moves easily over the jumps. Emma knows that if it wasn't for all the social action he was getting with the other horses, Tower would be plain bored. The jumps are raised to three feet six inches. This eliminates nine riders, leaving six, including Emma, who is laughing to herself. She knows Tower is showing off. Now the jump is raised to three feet nine inches. On the final go-round, all but two horses clear the jumps, including Tower.

On the second to the last jump, Emma loses a stirrup. But she stays in the saddle, avoiding a potential fall. Her seat is secure. A flapping stirrup distracted Tower. He clips the top rail, dislodging it. Emma is in second place. She tells Tower it is not his fault. She collects her red ribbon and waves it at her mother, who is sitting up in the third row of bleachers, and then up at Jules, who is standing by his parents now, in the row behind. He is smiling and waving back at her. Emma is trotting toward the far exit gate when she receives a picture from Tower. *He wants to jump the perimeter fence.* He sends her a picture of him clearing the rail. "Oh, my God," gasps Emma. But she loosens up on the reins just slightly, squeezes with her legs, and Tower breaks into a canter, then a hand gallop, and the fence is right there. Emma braces for the takeoff, and Tower is airborne and easily clears the fence, exactly as he showed her he would.

Spectators are standing now, shocked. Then, shouting and applause. The announcer says, "Well, folks, that's one way to exit the arena. But I don't suggest anybody else try it! That's a five-foot fence."

Emma circles Tower around and walks him back through the parked cars. She is exhausted and amazed. She is stunned at how easy that jump was. Tower had sent her the image of him jumping. She just *had* to go. It was *his* call. All she had to do was ride. Jules is there now, slapping Tower on the neck, and beaming up at Emma, and he shouts, "Awesome!"

* * *

That night, while word of the jump floods Malibu, Emma is sitting at the kitchen table with her parents.

"So," says Allan, "you took Tower over a five-foot fence. A steel pipe fence at that!"

"Tower, he told me."

"And you should have seen the crowd," Millie adds, clasping her hands in excitement. "They loved it. They say nobody has ever jumped that fence. I was *sooo* proud of you, Emma. You looked so beautiful, so … natural."

"Thanks, Mom."

"You could have also broken your neck," says Allan. "That's not a fall-down jump! It's a solid *fence!*"

"Tower said it okay."

Allan purses his lips, shakes his head. "So when do horses tell people what to do? We tell them what to do. We are their *master!*"

"He … showed me the picture."

Allan rolls his eyes. He has heard all this picture stuff before. Frustration rising like acid reflux, he snaps, "Okay. But if Tower says he'd like to jump over four lanes of traffic on Pacific Coast Highway, give him a firm *no* on that!"

Emma nods, falling silent now, overwhelmed by her father's outburst.

They finish supper. Emma goes to bed.

Allan and Millie sit in front of the television. They pretend to watch.

"I don't like the way this is going," says Allan. "That girl *will* get hurt. She could die!"

"She's a good rider," Millie says reassuringly.

"Good riders get killed when horses jump four feet over five-foot *solid* fences."

"Can't argue with that."

"We have to do something," Allan growls.

"Like what?"

"Like … get her back to a specialist."

"Okay," Millie says, irritated now. "We'll do a follow-up. Been a while. You know, we're not alone in this. They say 750,000 Americans have autism. Might even be millions."

"Yeah, well, what I want to know is if this condition is so prevalent, why is there no cure? Why do we not know what it is? Where did it come from?"

"Some people say it is caused by vaccines – all those drugs we use to make sure our children do not get all those very old diseases. But that's not proven."

"So, we have vaccinated Emma for every disease available on the planet," says Allan.

"According to current medical wisdom, that was the right thing to do."

Silence falls, then Millie says, "What I notice is that Emma's symptoms seem to decline the more she is involved with horses, especially Tower. There is something so … special about her relationship with that horse. Ever notice when she is talking with Tower, she sounds normal? She sounds strange only when she is talking with people, us included."

Allan puts his hand on Millie's arm. "I just … don't want anything to happen to her."

"I know."

Then, after a long silence, he says, "That *is* a five-foot fence they cleared. Now that's a fence you'd find in Grand Prix jumping … I must admit, I'm impressed. Terrified, but impressed."

Millie pats him on the shoulder.

Then Allan adds, "But we should take her back to the specialist, somebody who can really tell us what is going on. I can't have Emma put in danger because of some crazy pictures a horse is sending her."

Millie stops patting his shoulder.

CHAPTER TEN

Monday, April 5. The Armbrust ranch. Millie is throwing clothes in the washing machine. Allan is repairing a fence. Emma is at school. Millie's cell phone rings. She frowns. She doesn't recognize the number. She snaps the phone shut. Wrong number, she thinks. Moments later it rings again. Same number. This time she answers, and she hears a familiar voice. It is very British, very cultured. "Hello there, darling. I'm in town, so I thought I'd pop over for some tea and cucumber sandwiches."

"Harry, my God. It's you!"

"No, it's not God. It's just Harry. Although if I get this big acting job, *I will* be God!"

Millie feels both fear and a dangerous rush of sheer joy. She flashes on memories of being with Harry, the incredible romance, made even more precious by its stolen, illicit nature. She was, after all, married to Allan at that time. She desperately wants to see Harry again, and she desperately does *not* want to see him again – ever.

"Hey," he continues, "I'm just down the road at Islands. Drop in and I'll buy you a burger and fries. I want to see you. I'd be happy with a few minutes!"

Millie hears herself say, "Okay, Studly,… I mean, Harry, I'll see you in half an hour."

"Hey," he says, joy in his voice, like a man with a happy tune playing in his head, "Studly works for me!"

The moment she hangs up, she wishes she hadn't taken the call. "Oh, how I *hate* cell phones!" Millie says to nobody.

CHAPTER ELEVEN

Monday, April 12. Allan and Millie Armbrust are sitting in the austere office of Jacob Rosenthal, MD, a UCLA specialist in autism and neurology, but also, by personal interest, a student of animal behavior. A politically powerful friend secured this appointment at short notice. Dr. Rosenthal owns horses, on a sport level, and has published papers regarding the differences between the brains of animals and the brains of humans. He is observing Emma's EKG, EEGs, an MRI, and reports from various specialists who have examined her since she was a child. He has studied them.

"Your daughter," he says, "is autistic."

"Yes," says Millie, "we've known that practically since she was born."

Allan nods, then quickly adds, "But it is not severe."

Too quickly, thinks Dr. Rosenthal. *This could be a combative parent.* He regards Allan with new interest, but says nothing.

"So we have been told," says Millie.

"But nobody has given us a cause," says Allan.

"Ah," says Dr. Rosenthal, "that's because we do not know the cause. Some blame vaccines. I strongly doubt that. Others blame early parenting, you know, the mother didn't show enough love. I don't wear that either. Another theory: the ancestors of modern man moved from Africa 80,000 years ago and met with Neanderthals, probably somewhere in the Middle East, and besides killing them, they also procreated with them. By lining up the Neanderthal genome with DNA from humans and chimpanzees, scientists have identified some small changes that are unique to humans. Some were in genes involved in energy metabolism, and others could have been the start of Down syndrome and autism. It's a stretch, but we do know autism has been around a long, long time. I've read research by John Hawks at the University of Wisconsin, and he says that with absolute certainty, modern man has these Neanderthal genes."

Millie leans forward, as if to offer something, but changes her mind. In her heart, she *knows* she has been a good mother. And she has never met a Neanderthal!

Dr. Rosenthal consults the papers again. "I see Emma was normal, but then you noticed at age two, she didn't communicate like other babies, and going forward, that didn't appear to change. And she didn't like to be with other children."

"Yes, that's true. But later on, she improved at school, playing somewhat with other kids. And down the road from our ranch, there were a brother and sister, Jules and Suzanne. She liked being with them, played there all the time."

"You reported she always seemed happy, but in her own way," ventures Dr. Rosenthal, flicking papers.

"True. She would rather be with animals than people. And that ... is still true. She didn't like to be touched, either. Except by animals. Dogs can lick her all day long, and horses can slobber on her. But she is happy. You know, she *never* cries."

"Never cried. Not ever?"

"Not ever."

"Well, this is certainly consistent with autism," Dr. Rosenthal declares.

Allan taps the desk lightly with his fingers. Dr. Rosenthal takes note of the tap, tap, tap. He consults his notes again. "You report here that Emma was especially sensitive to noise and light, that she could always hear and see things you or Allan could not."

"Yes," says Millie, "that's true. We put a fluorescent light in her room when she was a little girl, and we had to take it out, because she could hear a humming and could see a flicker in the light that unsettled her. We couldn't hear or see anything unusual with that light."

"Let me explain what I have observed," says Dr. Rosenthal as he swivels around in his chair. He presses a button on a control panel, dropping a screen on a wall behind his desk. He touches more buttons. Lights dim. On the screen is an enlarged picture of Emma's brain.

Dr. Rosenthal points with his laser at the top of the brain. "This," he says, "is the site of the frontal lobes, the leading edge of the neocortex, which sits behind the forehead. This part of the brain actually has six layers and encompasses the cerebral cortex. It wraps around the subcortical, also known as the lower brain structure. Now, notice the shadow there. It's uneven. Darker areas indicate less function. Part of the neocortex is functioning okay, other parts not so well. This is the part of the brain that takes in most of the information we receive, mostly by sight and sound. It handles our intellect, like reading, reasoning, philosophy, all that refined thinking. This is the part of the brain we use when we write books about all the other parts of the brain we are trying to understand."

Millie and Allan look at the screen with fixed attention.

"Emma has a neocortex and frontal lobes that appear to function minimally. There are irregular cortical laminar patterns in the frontal lobe."

Dr. Rosenthal moves his laser to an area lower on Emma's skull.

"This," he says, "is the area of the middle brain, or the paleomammalian brain. It has to do with social function. In the evolution of man, millions of years ago, it came before the frontal lobes. Back when man lived in packs, this is the brain he used to figure out where he was in that pack. It helped him establish the order of his presence, gave him a sense of being."

He lowers his laser and takes a deep breath. "Now this," he says, "is what is commonly called the *reptilian brain. It is man's oldest brain. Basically, it controls the body's unconscious functions, as well as breathing and reaction to sudden danger. Its role is like a last-ditch stand: if all else fails, this makes us react instinctively to danger. Come up behind somebody, fire a gun, he or she will drop to a fetal position instantly. This is not a reasoned response to danger. It is immediate, triggered by the reptilian brain. This brain has been with man since the beginning of his time, maybe 6 million years. Some researchers say 95 percent of man's DNA today was carried by primates 65 million years ago. I don't know exactly what that means, though. DNA is like a row of switches; it depends what switches are turned on at the time."*

Dr. Rosenthal rocks back in his chair, letting the information fall where it may. "It was nature's way, as man developed, to throw nothing away. As man evolved and needed to sort himself out among other creatures, a new brain evolved over the old brain. And then, through millions of more years, he developed tools and began to communicate more precisely, first in sounds and then words. The frontal lobes developed to handle ever-increasing complexities of life, the most complex being communication. Most importantly, the electromagnetic energy produced by his brain changed, making it less sensitive to the electromagnetic energy produced by lower animals, such as horses and dogs. This was the start of a very slow disconnect between preman and animals, and modern man and animals – except for some people. But we'll get to that."

He waits a moment. "Our brain grew a bit like a small farmhouse, where rooms are added as more kids arrive. Brain mass was added, but not taken away, and each new addition remained connected to existing structures. We know a lot more about the brain than we used to, but there is a lot we do not know. The theory is that we have three brains, each independent of the other, but connected. Within all of us is the brain of an animal, this lower reptilian brain, still capable of producing electromagnetic frequency at levels millions of years old."

Dr. Rosenthal gathers his thoughts and then continues, "Electromagnetic energy produced by animals, such as a horse, and the energy produced by somebody with a brain like Emma's, with its particular wiring, could be so sensitive as to be completely interactive, meaning one brain could read the other brain."

He pauses and then continues, "People with full functioning neocortex and generous frontal lobes are smart in intellectual ways, but they are not as well-connected to the other, more primitive parts of their brain because they don't need to be. It's the old 'use it or lose it' cliché. The world of intelligent people is a world of words, philosophy, and building on blocks of reason. That's what makes them intelligent, according to the common standard. The brain of these individuals is a busy place indeed! Imagine a city skyline at night, all that power running everything, making all those lights. The healthy, modern brain of an intelligent person is a microcosm of this."

Allan shakes his head, both in frustration and interest. "So, what are you saying here in regard to Emma? Is she stupid? Is she not intelligent? You're saying … her brain lights are … off?"

Dr. Rosenthal purses his lips and looks away from the projected image. He was right. Allan is going to be difficult.

Then he sighs and moves forward. "We already know that Emma is more comfortable with images than words. She finds it difficult to put words in the sequences other people do naturally. This makes her shy, not antisocial, but always guarding against being with people she does not know. And it certainly doesn't make her stupid! She's just … different. And in her own way, very intelligent!" He flips charts. "These tests show she doesn't like loud noises, as you discovered very early. They are to her like a very bright light is to us. The human environment in which she lives is structured for normal people experiencing reasonable exposure to sound and light, with words dominating almost every interaction. That is sensory overload for Emma."

Millie smiles. "Yeah, we bought her a dog whistle once so she could train a new dog. She blew it one time. Said it hurt her ears!"

"How did she do with the dog training?"

Millie laughs. "The dog did everything she asked. She never used the whistle. The dog just knew what she wanted."

Silence fills the room, save for the ticking of a large, ornate grandfather clock against the wall. Tick, tick, tick.

Dr. Rosenthal continues, happy now that the mood seems to be lightening. "Emma is more comfortable with images because that is how her sensory intake works. She sees her environment in pictures, like a never-ending slide show, powered by her particular electromagnetic energy. She sees every little detail in the whole picture, whereas normal people just see the whole picture. Well, this is how most animals see the world, especially horses. They use that very old brain similar to our old brain – which we rarely use. Because for a million years, we haven't had to use that brain regularly. Most people go years without using the reptilian brain. But the wiring is still there! Emma is using it constantly, every awake moment. She is generating electromagnetic energy that horses are sensitive to. They "read" her signals. This part of her brain is working constantly when she is awake – and when she sleeps. When Emma looks at an object, she sees exactly what the horse sees. But what is most important is the horse – in this case, Tower – and Tower know lets her know she is exchanging pictures with him. Their electromagnetic fields are compatible.

"This is how horses communicate with each other. They exchange energy, and there is a strong theory this is in pictures. They supplement this communication with posturing, noise, attitude. Just like we use words to communicate with each other, horses use images transmitted with electrical brain-generated energy. Emma is that very, very rare person who is in that same communication loop. She is not comfortable in our world, but she is totally comfortable in the world of the horse. Ancient parts of her brain are as highly developed as the frontal lobes and large neocortex of our brains. Her brain is wired differently from our brain … but it is in tune with the wiring of the brain of the horse."

The clock on the wall chimes four times. Dr. Rosenthal takes a deep breath and presses forward. "It can be argued that our highly-developed frontal lobes might explain why normal people are so vulnerable to brain damage or dysfunction. Animals do not appear to have this exposure – but then, would we recognize mental illness in a horse? The price normal people pay for having such 'big, fat frontal lobes' is they become oblivious in ways animals and autistic people are not."

He sighs, the weight of the subject showing on his face. "It is true we know only a fraction of what there is to know about the human brain. We know even less about the autistic brain. Autistic persons process information in a fundamentally unique way. The difference is that the electromagnetic energy produced by their brain and central nervous system is sufficiently powerful for them to be on the same electrical grid as 'lower' animals, like dogs, cats, and in Emma's case, her horse, her animal of choice.

Autistic persons process information inwardly in a manner that does not seem, to them, to need words or all the trimmings of 'normal verbal human socialization.' They emit a different electromagnetic energy that can be perceived and interpreted with extreme sensitivity by other animals generating similar frequencies – but not by 'normal' human beings. This energy can also travel a long, long way. And there are theories that it never vanishes and it does not adhere to the confines of space or time, as we know it."

Millie's eyes widen, and she leans forward. The words gush out. "Yes, yes, Allan has told me stories about when he was growing up in the Australian Outback on his family's cattle property, and feral aboriginals would communicate with each other over hundreds of miles."

"Yeah," says Allan, "but that was normal, for them. After all, they were savages. Couldn't even speak English! Running around the bush wearing loincloths and carrying spears! Bloody wild, they were!"

Millie shoots him a glance.

Allan glares back at her, "Well, they were savages. They could use that power to kill. And they did. Was always one badass in the mob who could point the bone, tell somebody the tribe didn't like that he was gonna die, and he would! We tried to save a lot of them, flew them to Cairns Base Hospital, plugged them into modern medicine, but they just died anyhow."

"Sounds pretty advanced for a million-year-old power," observes Dr. Rosenthal.

"Hey, don't forget," counters Allan defensively, "we had trucks. They didn't. We listened to the BBC. We were at least civilized." He takes a deep breath, then adds solemnly: "But we couldn't save those darkies from the pouripouri of the witch doctor."

"You're right," says Dr. Rosenthal, rolling his eyes. After a while, he explains, "Okay, it makes sense, this way of communication the aboriginals possessed. Given their isolation and great distances between each other, it is highly possible – probable, I'd say – that they developed an enhanced sense of ESP, the use of nonverbal electromagnetic communication. They did this because they had to. No cell phones back then, right? Ah, the evolving brain, a wondrous thing!"

He pauses and then continues, "I have to tell you about bloodhounds. They have been shown to follow tracks over three hundred days old, detecting the scent of a person from just the sweat deposited in the sole of a walking shoe. This makes their sense of 'smell' about five thousand times stronger than that of a human. If one translates the enhancement of smell in a bloodhound to increased sensitivity of a horse to electromagnetic signals perceived in a human brain, the implications are enormous in understanding how somebody like Emma can communicate with a horse."

"Yeah," says Allan, "but is this some new-era green, fuzzy-wuzzy science?"

Dr. Rosenthal looks surprised. "It's actually very old science. The man who pioneered it was Hans Berger, over a hundred years ago."

Dr. Rosenthal tells the story of Berger, who had planned to become an astronomer and was serving in the German army in the 1890s when his horse slipped down an embankment. Berger was knocked out, and then woke, realizing he was seriously injured. Meanwhile, his sister, who lived many miles away, had a sudden feeling he was in trouble. She saw in her mind a picture of him injured, in a location she could see very clearly. She ran to her father, who telegraphed his son's army unit, and they searched for him, found him exactly where his sister had described, and saved his life. Berger was so astonished by the transmission of this message from his brain to his sister's brain that he gave up looking at the stars, and instead started researching electromagnetic impulses in the human brain. He fathered EEG and EKG."

Dr. Rosenthal adds, "Lord knows where he would have gone with the subject, had he not died … unexpectedly."

Dr. Rosenthal shakes his head, as if to brush off an unpleasant thought, and then continues, "Still today, we know more about what is on Mars than what is in our brain. And we know even less about the brain of the horse. But I am totally convinced they can read our electromagnetic energy – and that very few of us can get on their electrical grid."

Allan shakes his head. "Hey, man has been riding the horse a long time, just about forever. We must have learned something!"

"Sure," says Dr. Rosenthal, "but consider the horse has been around, in some form or another, for about 55 million years. Now let's say that time represents one mile. Man has been riding horses for about five thousand years. This means we have been riding the horse for 6.25 inches of that one mile. The horse has learned a lot more about us than we have about him! Why? It has been in his interest to do so!"

Allan shakes his head but says nothing.

Dr. Rosenthal continues, "So, do question anybody who tells you they know everything about horses. Now Emma, she knows more than most horse trainers will ever know, because her wiring is equine compatible."

"Yeah, but how does this happen?" Allan asks, frowning.

Dr. Rosenthal smiles. "Let me offer another analogy. Strike a tuning fork to make the sound of concert A. Let's assume the brain of the horse is tuned to concert A. And then let us assume Emma's electromagnetic output is also tuned to concert A. When she is in communication with a horse, the frequency would be identical to that of the horse. It would sound like a single note – concert A."

Allan is incredulous. "You mean … she can *talk* with horses and they can *talk* with her … because they're in tune?"

"Yes."

"Makes no sense at all to me," Allan snaps.

"Does it have to?"

"Yes. Sounds like a fairy tale."

Silence settles heavily on the desk, a bridge of doubt between the two men.

"Well," says Allan after a while, "just how are these pictures, energy, whatever, transmitted?"

"We don't know. We just know they are."

"I don't believe it," says Allan. "If we don't know how they are being transmitted, then we can't believe they are being transmitted."

Another silence. Eventually Dr. Rosenthal sighs and says, "Point taken. But at this time, we also do not know how sound waves travel. We can simply monitor and measure them, and control them. We do not know how electricity travels either, but we can measure and harness that as well. We do not deny the existence of sound or electricity because we do not know how it works, because while we can control those forces, we do not much care. We're too busy using them. We don't even know how gravity works, but we do know that an apple that falls from a tree belongs thereafter on the ground, or wherever it comes to rest, until somebody or some force moves it."

"And your point is …?" Allan asks.

"My point is Emma can receive and transmit 'pictures' with horses. Don't know how she does it, but she most certainly does. I believe these images are electromagnetically generated on a grid common to her and the horse."

He pauses and smiles. "You know, I used to sail yachts long distances, alone. It always amazed me how I heard voices, and music, especially late at night, when there was no apparent source for the sound, just the unique, dense quiet of a very large ocean. It was often old-style sailor music, or the kind of laughing you would hear from a party on a passing ship. I became so accustomed to the noise on transoceanic journeys, I ignored it; it was audible wallpaper. When it was especially quiet, I saw an image of a pirate, standing up there on the bow, hanging onto the halyard. The first time I saw him, he was so real I called out and asked him what the hell he was doing on my boat. He immediately vanished. And yes, he came back several times, a picture so clear, down to the last detail, the gilded handle of his sword, the rose patterns on the red scarf about his waist."

Dr. Rosenthal smiles. "I ignored him as well. The nightly picture just became … normal."

Millie says, "It … seems … such a strange thing, so hard to grasp. Our Emma communicating on such a strange, precise level …"

Dr. Rosenthal nods. "It's a fact of nature. If you believe it, you do not need an explanation. If you do not believe, no acceptable explanation is possible."

Allan takes a deep breath, and then announces, "I want Emma normal."

Dr. Rosenthal raises his eyebrows. "Now that's an interesting word – 'normal.' I'd like somebody to tell me what is 'normal' for a person."

"That's easy," says Allan quickly. "It's somebody who doesn't talk with horses!"

The clock chimes, and Dr. Rosenthal considers its face, as if puzzled by the numbers, then announces, "Okay, we have gone far enough today. Let me check my schedule." He consults a calendar on his desk. "I need to see you as soon as possible so we do not lose this train of thought. I have another commitment now. So ... Wednesday, April 21, okay? I have much to tell you. And we have decisions to make, and alternatives to consider."

"Alternatives?" Allan asks. "Like what?"

"There's medication. But let's discuss that another time."

"Finally, some real modern science is kicking in," Allan offers, his tone upbeat.

Dr. Rosenthal lets it go, sees the couple out, closes the door, and then leans against the wall. He runs fingers through his thinning hair and rubs his temples. Where he would go with the next meeting would be crucial to Emma's survival.

CHAPTER TWELVE

Sunday, April 18. Emma has rushed through her chores, saddling Tower so fast they hardly talk.

She gallops up the hills now, past where the lioness had been, and up through a little-used path leading to the waterfall. This is now their favorite place, hidden from the chaos down on Kanan Road. This is where time is suspended and they are alone in a world full of cricket noises, chirping birds, gurgling water, and the flop of leaping frogs. Always Jules has a new story about when they were kids. And always, a history book.

Every time Emma sees Jules now, her stomach twitches; but when he talks, she feels warmth and a calmness – a sense that everything about this is good, very good. She marvels at how easily he handles horses. Suzanne's horses are always hard to trailer load, but Jules loads them for the Trancas show so easily. He just throws the lead rope over the neck and looks to where he wants the horse to go. They jump right in. They know what he wants.

Emma wonders if Jules also exchanges pictures with horses. Or maybe he just knows horses and does not need to exchange pictures.

Emma is riding along now, anxious to meet Jules as planned, at the waterfall. She thinks about those visions that keep coming at night, especially when he reads her Gothic books. Zehun is always there now, in some new place, and she is so relaxed with him. She feels overwhelming warmth in his strength, and a gentleness that is, she concludes, even more soft than the wings of a butterfly. But she is confused, because Zehun and Jules are like the same man, but in different places, in different times. When she is with Zehun, she can't help but think of Jules. And when she is with Jules, she can't help but think of Zehun. But these images make the meetings even more exciting. Still, she feels troubled by the excitement. Is this wrong?

Zehun has ventured into her soul at depths far greater than has Jules. She wonders too about this, and is troubled by the difference. She sometimes feels it is Zehun who is urging on Jules, making him more bold, just like himself, but first trying to teach him to be gentle. She becomes carried away with the images hidden in her bedroom; they are a trigger to an excitement she craves, a safe place to be, an incredibly romantic otherworld. What she experiences with Zehun is so powerful, always so dangerous, yet deeply fulfilling. Amid all the chaos, Zehun is there for her, always with his strong arms, his gentle ways. Now Jules, he has touched her in her dreams, but not to the same depth as has Zehun. When Jules touches her in reality, however, she shivers with joy. Fire pours from his fingertips. She finds herself surrendering to Jules, but in her imagination only. Passion with Jules always surrenders at a certain, safe place. Zehun, on the other hand, always thrusts forward, purposeful, bold, yet gentle. He cradles her heart in his hand as gently as mist falls on a rose, as he plunders deep inside her.

Emma feels Tower toss his head, the reins pulling through her fingers. He has heard something. She is jerked back to reality. Now she suspects he is also irritated by her roving thoughts. She dismisses all images of Zehun. This is Tower's time, after all! Zehun would be too much of a distraction. Her soul is charged by Tower's massive energy.

Emma hears the waterfall at the same time she hears Jules trotting up the trail. His smile causes her heart to skip a beat.

"What a pleasure to run into *you*," he says, with joyous sarcasm Jules is riding Suzanne's regular horse Rose.

"Follow me," says Emma. Together they ride off though thick brush that suddenly opens out to a pond about an acre in area, fed by the waterfall snaking its way down a fifty-foot rock face. They dismount here, securing the horses to a tree.

Jules goes to his saddlebag and pulls out a book. "Just like old times," he says. "Here, let me read you something about Alexander the Great."

And so he reads, then he reviews what he read. "Alexander used horses, but he was gentle with them. He was the first to start using horses in sports, started them racing in the Olympics. Can you believe that was about 2,500 years ago?"

Emma is absolutely enthralled to be entertained like this. She looks up at Jules and wonders how he is so different from all the other boys she knows, so intelligent, so ... romantic.

"Now here," says Jules, flipping forward through the pages, "this is my favorite character, Attila the Hun. You know, *you* have the power that he had." He looks across at the horses haltered to a tree. "Attila knew what they were thinking. He could communicate with them, just like you do. You do what the Huns did."

"It's easy," says Emma.

Jules laughs. "For you, yes."

Emma smiles. "Okay, tell me when Attila wanted to marry the beautiful sister of the governor of Constantinople. I *like* that."

He reads. Emma lies back, smelling the earth, soaking in Jules's words.

After a while, Jules puts down the book and goes back to his saddlebag and brings out sandwiches. "A picnic," he explains.

They sit by each other, closer now than before. Emma smiles deep inside herself, marveling at how this reality so exactly parallels her constant thoughts of Zehun. So close, in fact, that she worries now that this might not be real, that it might also be just a vision. Would he touch her now, as Zehun did? Would he turn suddenly into that warrior who was always in those visions? She is at once confused and warm with happiness. She looks at Tower, haltered to a tree there by Rose. He is kind of dozing, his tail automatically swiping flies off his rump. He sends no pictures, his transmitter off.

Emma looks at Jules and again she asks, "How do I *really* know you?"

"We were together a lot as kids, remember?"

"I remember some."

"I went to your place too. Me and Suzanne. We had sleepovers. I used to read you stories about horses from my history books."

Emma nods. Now all is clear. "But I see you other places. Faraway, strange places, another time. Many horses, many people, dressed, like, old ways."

He looks at her for a long while, and then he says, "I don't know. I have seen you only where I have seen you. But sometimes I look at your horse, and I see a picture of you there. Jumping. Galloping. Laughing. That horse really likes you."

He looks at Tower and then adds, "But he sees nothing now. I think he is asleep."

Emma replies, "He's ignoring us."

The waterfall gurgles, and a light breeze rustles branches. The sun is sending its last rays over the horizon. Somewhere an owl hoots. Emma is feeling a soft warmth on her hand. She looks down. Jules is gently holding her hand. Emma is aware of this warmth spreading up her arm and deep into her body, a soft current. She gasps, and realizes she has forgotten to breathe.

"Are you all right?" Jules asks.

"Oh yes, oh yes," she says, squeezing his hand now, and all at once is suddenly alarmed. She has never before squeezed a boy's hand. Not here, not in real time. Of course, Zehun has done that – and a lot more! The thought of somebody touching her has always terrified her, but with Jules – and Zehun – it is somehow different. Zehun is in another place, where her words to him come as if from the people around her in real time, here in Malibu. Complete sentences, and fluctuations in tone. No tape recorder pattern in the land of Zehun! In *that* faraway world, she is what her father would call "normal." She dismisses this observation, and concentrates now on the feel of Jules's hand.

And for many minutes they sit now, contemplating the fading day.

"I want to stay like this forever," she says, turning to look into his incredible eyes.

He squeezes her hand again. "We will be like this, forever. I know."

This time she squeezes back, and an amazing heat rises up through her body. She feels her heart pounding, like it is racing out of control. A human hand in her hand! She is amazed she feels no terror. And this is real, not like with Zehun, in that other world far away and long ago.

And then he stands, lifts her to her feet, and ever so slowly pulls her to him. Emma feels the warmth of his body against her from head to toe. Together, they are locked in a warm place. Emma has never been held like this. At least, not in this real world, the world with all the noise and the lights and the people who put words in sequences she finds strange. She has felt this warmth with Zehun. But that is another world. She knows she is trembling now, and hopes Jules does not feel this.

"Are … you all right?" Jules asks. "You look pale."

Emma's head snaps up. "Yes," she says. "Just tired. We go now."

Jules holds her at arm's length and gently demands, "First, tell me about your visions."

She looks at him for the longest time, then says, "They real. And Zehun real when I visit him. He looks like you. Zehun is warrior."

For a moment, Jules is taken aback. He composes himself and says, "Well, that's good. I always fancy myself as a warrior. What sort of warrior am I – as Zehun?"

"Attila thinks you best. You his first lieutenant."

"I must be bloodthirsty if he thinks that."

"Attila thinks you not enough bloodthirsty! You kill Romans. Many, all day! But you no kill women and children. Attila cannot understand why you no rape the women."

Jules considers this, and then says, "That must be a problem for Attila."

"Yes."

Jules moves to her now and takes her in his arms. "I have to say, I do not recall riding with Attila the Hun. I know of Attila, I read everything about him, but … but … he is history. This is now."

"You no understand."

"I'm trying, okay?"

He hugs her. Emma is alarmed again at how physical contact with this person does not make her feel uncomfortable.

Emma stops, and then she says, "Something else about Zehun."

Jules looks at her with his kind eyes, and she feels his great strength holding her shoulders. She searches desperately for words.

"What ... what is it?" Jules asks gently.

When no words come from Emma, Jules steps forward and holds her. "Tell me, please."

After a while, Emma says, "We go home now."

"It's about Zehun, right? You want to tell me something very special about him?"

Emma is silent for a long time. She is searching for words, but none come.

Jules shrugs, giving up this pursuit. "Okay," he says softly.

Jules helps Emma on her horse, mounts his own horse, and together they ride into the coming night, the beat of horse hooves the only sound.

A little farther up the trail, at a fork, Jules goes left, and Emma continues on down the hill, toward home. Just once she looks back. Jules is also stopped, looking back. Emma waves. Jules waves, then turns his horse.

Riding home, Emma ponders why she had not been honest with Jules. She should have told Jules about the love she has for Zehun, about what REALLY happened. But a little while later, she is feeling only Tower's warmth and greatness.

Tower sends her a picture of a full bucket of feed.

Riding home now, alone, bathed in the soft light of a rising moon, she puts aside her concerns and thinks of Jules, and Zehun, and how they are so much alike. How they are really the *same*, just in different places at different times. Now she knows she is smiling. Tonight, she will either dream of Jules or visit Zehun. Either one holds the promise of excitement.

CHAPTER THIRTEEN

Wednesday, April 21. Allan and Millie are back in the office of Dr. Rosenthal. They assume the same seats they had before. Dr. Rosenthal notes Allan looks more relaxed. He is encouraged by this, knowing what sensitive ground they must now cover. It will not be easy.

"We've been thinking a lot about what you said," says Millie. "It's a very big subject."

Dr. Rosenthal nods. "It is probably one of the biggest medical puzzles in the world right now."

Allan shakes his head. "I thought science had a handle on everything."

"Yeah, we wish," sighs Dr. Rosenthal. He shuffles papers on his desk, not wanting to rush. Then he continues, "What has happened with Emma is actually very natural. If we lose use of our right arm, it doesn't take us too long to become left-handed – because we must in order to survive."

The clock ticks.

Dr. Rosenthal smiles. "History is full of people who have 'talked' with horses." He tells the story of Isaac Murphy, a black, born in Fayette, Kentucky, in 1859. He rode as a jockey in his first race at age fourteen – and he went on to win 628 races out of 1412 starts, an amazing average win of 44 percent. He never used a whip or a spur. He explained that he simply "talked" with his horse and asked him to "get in front." He won the Kentucky Derby three times.

Dr. Rosenthal continues, "Now Emma, she was born with a brain wired differently from what is considered normal today – so nature took care of her survival. It wired the other parts of her brain, man's very oldest brain. This ancient brain structure is, in all respects, working wonderfully for Emma."

Dr. Rosenthal turns in his swivel chair and points back up at the screen.

"Now this," he continues, "this is very interesting. If you remove the large neocortex from the human brain, along with the middle brain, you would have a brain that is little different, physically, from the brain of a horse. But mass is not paramount. What is highly relevant is the neural interaction with other portions of the brain, principally the temporal lobe, cerebellum, limbic system, and other connectivity."

Silence fills the room.

"And you know, I believe, millions of years ago, what Emma is experiencing today was normal. There was no word language. Just sounds, grunts, murmurs, screams, gestures, posturing. We hear these primitive sounds and gestures today from children with severe autism. Their language is unique. For humans, words came much later in their – our – evolution. The neocortex and the frontal lobes developed and wired up to handle this change. Autism remains a very deep mystery despite all the studies. Perhaps it will never be fully understood. I believe it has been around as long as humans have been around. The biggest thing modern medicine has done is give it a name – autism. And turned it into an industry."

Allan sighs heavily, his frustration so clear it is almost visible. He says, "But we don't live in ancient times. We live now, in Malibu, California. We are not in some bat-infested cave. Emma can't live like that. We have to do something!"

Dr. Rosenthal looks surprised. "Do what? Why? Emma is not ill; she is not unhappy. In fact, I would say, when she is with her horse, she is very happy. She has learned to 'handle' the other world – which is our world – and she survives very well with her 'limitations.' For her, our world is not natural. It is the world of the horse that for her is natural. She is benefiting, also, from the widely documented ability of the horse as a healing influence. All domesticated animals comfort people, and, yes, often heal. It is well documented that dogs can forecast seizures in people. They can also detect cancer before scientific diagnosis. However, the horse is special, probably because of its size and the amount of electromagnetic energy it subsequently produces."

"It's not normal," says Allan glumly.

Dr. Rosenthal cocks his head thoughtfully. "Ah, there's that word again – 'normal'! If each of us is unique, then by definition none of us is normal."

Allan looks at him, but says nothing.

Dr. Rosenthal continues, "What is not common must be called rare by definition. However, Emma has a foot in both camps, so to speak. What she has is very, very rare. A gift, some would say. It is my view Emma has just enough autism to be triggering constant function in the old brain – and because of this, she is on the same cerebral page as the horse, producing a compatible electromagnetic energy. How that works, I have no idea. I just know it works. She probably has this to a degree with all animals. But not with most people – because we are out of the loop."

"But … it's still not normal," Allan repeated.

"Ah, there it is," exclaims the doctor, "that word 'normal'! What, one might ask, *is* normal? There are as many definitions of that word as there are people!"

He shakes his head, amused at the coming thought. "You know, Mozart and Beethoven would have been classified to some degree today as autistic. We must all be thankful that in 1770 they did not have brain-altering drugs! Think of the amazing music the world would have lost!"

Allan takes a deep breath. "With all the modern medicine around today, there must be something we can do!"

Dr. Rosenthal closes his eyes, runs fingers through thinning hair, and says, "Okay, there's always medication."

Millie frowns. "What kind of drugs?"

"Let me explain," says Dr. Rosenthal. He did not want to go here, but the parents of his patient had asked, so he must. "The brain," he says, "any brain, has the ability to release its own painkillers, called endorphins. This is nature's version of a heavy drug, like heroin or morphine. It is nature's way of taking care of sudden pain. Lose an arm or a foot, and you do not immediately feel pain. Endorphins take care of that instantly."

The doctor chuckles, trying to soften the mood. "You know all that stuff you hear about crazy people whipping each other and liking it? Well, it's true. They *do* like it. Pain releases endorphins. This causes pleasure. At least initially."

He pauses, and then continues, "I didn't mean to get off the subject, but a common medication today to treat alcohol, cocaine, or heroin addiction is the drug naltrexone, which is actually an opium antagonist. It blocks natural opiates in the brain. There are many similar drugs. The current theory is that autistic people have very high levels of natural opiate production in the brain. Because of their ready and easy supply of endorphins, they are happy in their own world. They do not want to be social because they do not *need* to be social. They do not know loneliness. I do not know everything about Emma's world – nobody does, except her. She has a whole world exclusive to her, and it is my belief she visits it frequently, for this is where she finds comfort. For Emma, and others like her, there is a private and vast world to which they alone have access. It is their salvation. They enjoy this exclusive world. They are self-contained, happy in this universe. Just like heroin addicts are happy in their world. Naltrexone can change that. It can stop the free flow of opiates. The end result is the patient becomes 'more social.' If we could make Emma more social with such a drug, she would be forced to start using more words and, eventually, full sentences. She would seek the company of others – this is called socializing. This would happen because she would *have* to make it happen. Her brain would make both the demands and the adjustment. At least, that is the premise."

"Is there a side effect to this drug?" Allan asks.

"There are," he says quietly, rising from his chair, "potential side effects to every drug. And there will probably be side effects to this drug. I have to warn you about that in no uncertain terms! We just might collapse her world as it is today. To Emma, her world now is perfect. It just does not appear perfect to those around her. Medication will most certainly change how her brain works. I am not sure exactly what that change will be. But she *will* be different."

"We accept that," says Allan. "Anything to make her ... normal."

"Okay, then. We'll start immediately. Strong doses at first, and then we'll taper off to the dosage that is just effective. Normally, drugs are started in low doses and then increased. With this one, I would like to do the reverse. If the impact is too severe, we can stop immediately. That way, time is on our side. Should see changes in a few weeks."

Allan and Millie rise from their chairs and turn toward the door. With his hand on the brass doorknob, Allan turns and asks, "What happened to Hans Berger, who first measured electricity output in the human brain?"

"Oh yes, poor old Hans Berger," says Dr. Rosenthal, smiling, as if recalling an old, dear friend. "When Hitler was coming into power, he replaced traditional medical services with National Socialism. 'Traditional' meaning in the days when the doctor with his black leather bag came to your house and held your hand and did what he could, in that old healer concept, which often worked because people *believed* they were being cured. Anyhow, Hans saw no room in socialized medicine for original thinkers, so he … hanged himself, on June 1, 1941. The world will never know what else he might have discovered."

"That's so sad," says Millie.

"Suicide is a cop-out," says Allan bluntly. "It means you've lost the argument because you've run out of things to say, so all you have left is a final statement to which nobody can reply. He just couldn't handle change."

Millie gives Allan a strange glance, as if surprised he would make such a deep statement.

Dr. Rosenthal has no response. He shrugs and writes on a pad. "Your prescription. We'll have another appointment in thirty days. You will start to see results before then."

CHAPTER FOURTEEN

Saturday, April 24. Millie and Harry are sitting on a bleacher at Zuma beach. They have seen each other for lunch three times. Millie has told herself not to be doing this, but always her heart overrules reason.

"So," asks Harry, "how's Emma after the last visit with the specialist?"

"She's on the medication."

"What change is supposed to happen?" Harry asks.

"She's supposed to get more social, more verbal, more … normal."

"Would you like that?"

"I don't know."

"How are you and Allan handling this?"

"He's all for the medication. But he's also frustrated and angry, and I don't like that. Sometimes I think our world is falling apart. And here's the strange thing. We are putting Emma on medication to try and make her 'normal,' and here we are all 'normal' and we have all these challenges. I'm married and I'm here with you and I'm thinking a whole bunch of scary things that I should not be thinking. Is that normal? Emma has no such stress. She's already happy – or at least she was. Now I think something is changing …"

"Maybe my being in the picture is not helping."

"Oh, no. I find you being in the picture a big help, a distraction. It is a conflict that has a payoff. It's like I need a break, some kind of relief from all this stuff – Emma's condition, the sad state of the ranch, money issues. It's all so … so much."

Harry suppresses an urge to hold her. They are, after all, in a public place.

They talk for an hour. Millie announces she must leave. Cars have stopped at a traffic light across the street. Customers are streaming out of Sherman's Place. Millie resists the urge to kiss Harry. The area is bumper to bumper with weekend beach traffic.

"You know," says Harry, "this is ridiculous. We should go someplace more private, like get a motel room!"

"That's what I would be really afraid of!"

"Can't we go back to old times?"

"It would not be right. But that does not mean I don't want to," says Millie.

And then Millie walks across the parking lot, climbs in her car, and drives home. She does not look back. There are tears in her eyes.

CHAPTER FIFTEEN

Saturday, May 15. Emma is on Tower in the main exercise arena of her home. She is jumping him. Manuel is moving the jumps on her instruction. He is doing this with some reluctance. He doesn't like Emma. He thinks she is "spoiled."

Allan and Millie are meeting with their attorney in nearby Thousand Oaks. Emma knows this because she saw the appointment scheduled on the kitchen planner. She noticed her mom and dad were in a glum mood when they drove off. She heard them arguing. This worries her.

Manuel sets the jump at three feet six inches, and Emma and Tower easily clear it. She instructs Manuel to move the bar up to four feet. Tower also easily clears that height. Emma tells him to move the jump to four feet six inches. Tower easily clears that too. But Emma feels strange – the pictures she is getting from Tower are not clear. She is receiving them, but she has to concentrate on the images. This bothers her. Emma notices now that Tower is paying a lot more attention to the jumps. She feels he is working, rather than transmitting pictures. Emma reaches deep within herself for control. Her balance feels off.

She instructs Manuel to move the jump to four feet, and when she looks at it on a go-round, it looks higher than four feet; it looks almost the height of the rail Tower cleared down at the Trancas Arena back in February – the jump that got all Malibu talking. But this now is very different, because it is a single pole – unlike the five-rail fence at the Trancas Arena. For Tower to clear this jump, he will have to *perceive* its height. There is nothing under the jump to give it depth. It will show up on the picture in his brain as a single horizontal line; to a human, something like a thin, narrow, glitch line on a computer screen. Tower clears the jump, but Emma receives no images. Emma is relieved, but there is a queasy feeling in her stomach. She is afraid, and now wants to get off the horse. She looks in horror at her hands. They are shaking. She has never felt like this before.

She is patting Tower's neck when she notices a car parked by the rail of the corral. A tall, gray-haired man steps out of the expensive-looking black sedan with tinted windows. Emma recognizes him, but does not know his name. She has seen him before, at Trancas horse shows. She sees a picture of him there, leaning on the rail, the same car in the background.

"Emma," he says, waving a friendly arm. "That is beautiful jumping!"

She looks at him, trying to put a name to his face.

"Oh, I'm Earl. Earl Holloway. You know my daughter Mary. She rides at Trancas."

Emma rides over closer to the rail. In her mind, she can see Mary now. Mary is never very friendly. Emma sees Mary whispering to a friend, talking behind a cupped hand, and they both burst into laughter. This is the image Emma recalls from Trancas. She tries not to remember Mary, and she doesn't remember Earl's name. But she bluffs. "Okay."

"So," says Earl, "how high can that horse jump?"

"Don't know," says Emma.

"I know about the Trancas jump. That's five and a half feet. Measured it myself. Could he jump that high today?"

"No more jumping today."

Earl had put a cigar in his mouth before the jump, and Emma notices now it still has not been lit. Earl seems to be looking off into space, and then he says, "You don't look well. Is everything all right?"

"Yes."

"Tower hasn't even broken a sweat. He's ready to go!" Earl exclaims.

Emma considers the jump and Tower follows her gaze, but now the image Emma is receiving back is fuzzy. Then she turns toward the gate, heading out.

Earl Holloway changes mouth corners with his cigar, turns, climbs into his car, and drives off, the cigar still unlit.

Emma has unsaddled Tower and is brushing him down when her parents come up the driveway. They stop.

"How is Tower?" asks Allan. He and Millie remain seated in the car, engine running.

"Fine."

Allan looks at the jump. "That jump looks easy. Are you just warming him up?"

Emma nods.

Allan and Millie continue on up the driveway and pull up in front of the main house.

"Well," says Allan, "I see the medication has not kicked in. She's still acting crazy. That girl's gonna kill herself."

"The doctor said it would start working about now," says Millie, getting out of the car and moving toward the front of the house. "But she is ... different, don't you think?"

"Maybe," he says. Then he stops and purses his lips, deep in thought. "Now that I think of it, she walked away from a lowly four-foot jump. Maybe she *is* getting smart!"

In the kitchen, Millie pours two glasses of wine. Together they sit, taking advantage of the private time. Emma, they know, will be with Tower for as long as they let her.

Millie says, "The lawyer is right. We can't hold onto this place much longer. We have refinanced three times. The mortgage is way over what we are bringing in. We can't refinance again. We're underwater. We've sold all but three horses ..."

"There's Blazing Light – he's looking good. Gonna put some miles on him next month."

"We need $8,000," says Millie, as if not hearing him. "And we need it by Wednesday."

Emma enters the kitchen, walks past Millie and Allan, not looking at them, not speaking. A moment later, her bedroom door slams so hard a picture falls off a wall in the hallway.

"What the hell is that all about?" Allan asks. He stands and starts down the hallway.

Millie stands and grabs his arm. "Let her be alone. If she wants to talk, she will."

Allan does not answer. He walks back into the kitchen. Then he notices the red light of the answering machine. He is thankful for that – at least a temporary break from bad vibes. He plays the messages, all debt collectors – except the last one, which rivets his attention. It is Earl Holloway. Allan calls back the number, and Earl picks up on the first ring.

The men exchange pleasantries, and then Earl asks, "Is Tower for sale?"

Allan is caught by surprise. "Of course not. That's Emma's horse."

"He'd make a good backup for Mary."

"Well, forget Tower. He's not for sale. Emma's kind of attached to him."

"Would $5,000 cash buy him?"

"Naw, don't think so …"

"What about $10,000 cash. That's a lot for a back-up horse."

"But Emma …"

"Tower is too much for her. I saw her on that horse today. She was so scared she was white as a sheet. She couldn't wait to get off that horse. She's gonna kill herself on Tower."

"Tower *is* a lot of horse," Allan admits.

"I will be over in two days with $15,000 – cash! No vet checks, no trial period. Done deal."

Allan hears himself say, "Done deal."

He cradles the phone and is all but laughing. "Can you believe that? *I just sold Tower for $15,000*. Cash! No vet, no papers, no trial period, no nothing! We're out of the fire!"

Millie is shocked. She takes a deep breath. "Is that a good idea?"

"It's the best one I have right now."

"Why don't you sell that Rolex you've been carrying around for years?"

Allan looks at the watch on his left wrist, as if seeing it there for the first time. "Yes, well, just maybe I'll need that another day – when I *really* need it!"

Millie shakes her head and walks away.

Meanwhile, Emma is in her room. She rushes for the lithographs and wants more than ever to see Zehun. She closes her eyes, but this time it seems to take forever. Finally she hears the hooves of a galloping horse. She is in a shelter, alone, when she realizes a man is calling her name. She knows the voice. It is Zehun!

"Emma! Emma!" he yells.

Emma scrambles from her bed and flings back the horsehide that covers the door opening. Dawn is breaking. There is a heavy mist. And there is Zehun, on his horse, and all around villagers are peering out of slits in doorways. "The Romans are coming," yells Zehun. "Here, grab my hand now!" She reaches up, and Zehun in one swift move, hoists her up behind his soft saddle. "We have to get out of here," he yells, and then at flat gallop he heads for the forest.

An hour later, they are on high ground, and Zehun swings his horse around. Way down below them, the village is burning.

"Curse the Romans!" Zehun yells. "They will kill everybody!"

Emma is horrified at the sight. "You saved me again," she says.

"It was close. I knew that is where they were headed."

Zehun climbs down from the horse and lowers Emma to the ground. "We'll rest the horse a while, and then continue north. I saw some horses get loose down there. With luck, some of them will run this way."

And he was right. A short while later, three horses burst up from the south. The trail is steep on either side, and the horses have no place to go. They stop, and – very carefully – Zehun secures the largest of them, a bay mare. He uses a rawhide rope he had attached to his soft saddle. With this he makes a loop around the nose of the horse, then back up over the mare's head, and knots it under her chin. He loops the remainder of the rope over her mane, to make reins. "Here," he says, "get on!"

They ride two hours, and then Zehun says, "We're going to circle back to the west. Some of my brothers are not far from here."

The sun is directly overhead when they meet up with about fifty Huns. They open ranks to let Zehun and Emma through. At first they greet Zehun warmly, but their mood changes when they see Emma.

"I see you've caught yourself some loot," says one, his grin showing a line of broken teeth.

"And you all better keep your eyes off her. She is with me. Now, bring me a saddle for her, and get her a sword and bow as well! And give me supplies. We're going to pick up with Attila's main force."

Without getting off her horse, Emma straps the sword around her waist, placing it where she notices Zehun has his sword. Then she slings the quiver of arrows over her back, and sets the bow over her shoulder. Zehun observes this with interest. "I see it has been a while since you've armed yourself! Now let's go!"

Again they gallop off. At one point, Zehun looks back at Emma and observes. "At least you can keep up!"

It's late afternoon. Zehun stops by a large expanse of water. "We'll stay here for the night. This is safe. The Romans are heading east, where there are more villages to plunder."

"So, what now?" asks Emma.

"I'll tell you what now," says Zehun. "Get down off that horse, and I am going to start teaching you how to use sword and bow. It was lucky I found you in that village. You would have been dead – or at least, wish you were dead!"

Until night falls, Zehun instructs her in swordplay. "You learn quickly," he observes. "Remember, every time you swing that blade, make like you are going to kill somebody! And never take your eyes off his eyes!"

It is dark when they finish working with the bow. Zehun nods in satisfaction. "You are a natural with the bow! But you need more arm for the sword!"

Zehun looks around as night settles on the forest. "We'll bed here and ride at dawn. No fire, but there is dried goat in the bag."

"Are ... we going to be all right?"

"Oh yeah," Zehun says, smiling now, the new moon catching the whiteness of his teeth.
"We're going to be just fine – you and me!"

Emma feels the warmth of his body against hers as they lie together under a horsehide blanket.

CHAPTER SIXTEEN

Wednesday, May 19. Millie and Allan are back in the office of Dr. Rosenthal for their third visit. They assume their usual seats. Dr. Rosenthal settles into his big leather chair, leans forward, and looks over his half-rims. "So," he asks, "how is it going?"

Allan speaks, even as Millie is trying to decide how to respond. "Going great, Doc. That stuff's kicking in. Now Emma's just like any other know-it-all bitchy teenage girl who hates her parents. We're stupid and she's a genius. She's even talking more, but the words have a bite. She slams doors and plays that God-awful music. I'd like to get her to slam the doors to the beat of the music, so it would blend in a little more, but what she plays is not music!"

Dr. Rosenthal nods, but says nothing. He notices Allan is rushing his words. He knew this was coming!

"She is changing," says Millie.

"But that's what you want, right?" Dr. Rosenthal asks. "You want change. You want … normal."

"Yeah," says Allan, "we want normal. I can deal with normal."

Dr. Rosenthal looks at Millie and then asks, "What do you want?"

"I want her happy," Millie responds. "I don't want change at any cost."

The ticking of the grandfather clock fills the silence in the room, and then after a while Dr. Rosenthal says, "But she has always been happy. You have told me that many times."

"We want normal," says Alan.

Millie lowers her head and is silent.

"Fine," says Dr. Rosenthal. "Stay the course."

CHAPTER SEVENTEEN

Friday, May 21. Emma is home from school. It is late afternoon. She is in the barn with Tower. She has the halter in her hand. She is staring at Tower and she is stunned. There is *no picture.* She sees only a horse looking back at her. She slips on the halter, and she notices her hands are shaking. Tower snorts as he receives the halter. He pins back his ears. He retreats into the corner of the stall. Emma pets him, and he relaxes. She leads him out of the barn and snaps him into the crossties. She fetches her grooming equipment and begins to brush him, and she notices he is starting to relax. In the pit of her stomach, that queasy feeling has returned. She is moving about the horse as if in a trance, just doing what she always does. Halter horse. Brush horse. Saddle horse. Tower keeps turning, looking back at her, watching her every move. Emma tightens the cinch and walks Tower out of the barn, toward the mounting block. It is like she is watching herself doing this from afar.

She climbs aboard and walks into the arena, aware that Manuel is there now, at the gate. She trots around the arena and she realizes she has to work to get into the rhythm of the horse. Again, she is moving as if conditioned to follow one move after the other. She feels strange and for a while she does not know what it is, because she has never felt this before. And then she identifies this feeling; it is fear. Suddenly, Tower stops. Emma takes a deep breath and kicks him, and he moves forward. Now she sees Manuel at the jump. It is set at three feet six – an easy jump, thinks Emma. She circles the arena, looking at the jump, and then she turns. At an extended trot, she lines up the jump and then pushes Tower into it. First Tower breaks into a canter, then back into an extended trot, and just when Emma thinks he is going to take the jump, he stops. Emma feels herself going off to the side, and Tower spins, as if startled to see her there in the corner of his eye. Next, Emma realizes she is on the ground, desperately clutching the reins. Tower freezes. Manuel is rushing to Emma now. He picks up her head.

"What ... what happened, miss?" he asks, his voice hesitating with disbelief.

"Don't know," says Emma. "Feeling bad."

"Breathe deep!"

"All right," she says, standing now, relieved she could actually do that. No broken bones. She looks at Tower. She sees a horse looking back at her.

"I don't think you should ride anymore today," says Manuel. "This does not look right."

Emma narrows her eyes and glares at him.

"Sorry," he offers.

Emma takes a deep breath. "Okay," she says, dusting off her breeches.

"Here, let me put Tower away," says Manuel.

She hands him the reins.

Emma watches him lead Tower toward the hosing racks. She wants to cry, but can't.

She walks over to Manuel, who has Tower back in the crossties, hosing him down.

"Manuel, please, favor. Do not tell."

Manuel looks at Emma. He is happy she is asking something of him. "Okay by me," he says. "Maybe … you are just having a bad day. It will all be better tomorrow."

That night, Emma locks herself in her room, looks at the drawer where the lithographs are, but does not open it. She feels strange, like she is outside of her body. She throws herself on the bed and cries herself to sleep. There are no visions. She knows something terrible is happening, but she does not know what. She thinks with great desperation about what she is doing that is new. And then it strikes her – the medication her mother said would help her. She didn't know she needed help. Her mother said they were vitamins.

* * *

Saturday, May 22. While Emma and her mother are at the mall, a truck and trailer arrives at the Armbrust farm. Tower is loaded and driven off the property.

CHAPTER EIGHTEEN

In the spring of the year 441, history records two dramatic discoveries that would forever boost fortunes for Attila and his brother, Bleda. It happened when Attila, Bleda, and Zehun finally reached the eastern banks of the Danube. Their army was badly bloodied, and the horses exhausted. For a whole year, they had plundered their way through the northern tribes of Sarmatia. For five years now, the brothers had charged at the head of ten thousand horsemen on a path of destruction north of the Black Sea, then through the Caucasus passes, on into Persia and the Roman provinces of Asia Minor and Syria.

The Hun brothers had never been defeated, but they suffered heavily when they failed to outrun the arrows of the Roman horse archers. They bled even more when they were forced to fight hand-to-hand with the far superior Roman swordsmen. Their forces had been cut in half. They decided to make camp and regroup. Bows had to be strung, arrows made, horses rested.

"Our horses gave out," Attila told Bleda, the younger of the two brothers. Both men wore blood-soaked deerskin, a long sword at the waist, a quiver of arrows on the back.

Zehun was also spattered with blood, but some of the blood was his own. A Roman short sword had got under his guard while he was dispatching other Romans. His left arm was slashed. Attila observed this and said, "Fortunately, the Gods born you right-handed!"

"It's not deep," said Zehun.

Attila barked an order, and one of his always-present assistants appeared with a salve to rub on Zehun's wound.

Attila sighed and sat down. He unsheathed his sword and started drawing a stick figure of a horse in the dirt. He pointed the tip of the sword to the center of the back, equidistant between the front legs and the back legs. "This," he announced, "is where our horses give out."

"Perhaps we should all go on a diet," observed Bleda, always the comedian.

Attila answered with a scowl. He had no great love for Bleda, but gave him the benefit of the doubt. They were, after all, brothers.

Now Attila addressed Zehun. "You fought well today, my lieutenant. I saw you personally cut down a score of Romans! Unfortunately, it was not enough. Our losses have been heavy."

"I *hate* Romans," Zehun said.

"Well, keep fighting. Your reward will come. Rape and plunder!"

Zehun shot him a glance. "I live to kill Romans, not rape defenseless villagers."

Attila leveled a steady glare. "You do not understand. The world fears us because of what they call … terror. Killing people is not cruel. It is just what has to happen to instill fear. People in fear are much easier to defeat than people who have no fear. So, we must instill fear, real fear. It makes success certain. It cannot be done any other way. I want the world to *fear* us, not *love* us, and then we can do what we want, because people will be frozen with fear. Very simple."

Zehun considered this. "Is there no other way?"

Attila responded, "Not if you want to control them. If you can instill fear, it is much more powerful than the sword. Saves energy. Now I do recall you cut down the Leopard Man so you might spare the life of that girl peasant. Very ... interesting. She was of no value, but Leopard Man, he had skills. Could have used him these last few months."

"I am sorry he was not here. But I am not sorry I killed him."

Attila leveled another glare. "You killed him over that worthless girl. I would much rather she died than Leopard Man. He had much value. She has none."

Zehun takes a deep breath, knowing he is going into dangerous territory. "Her name is Emma, and I have made her my woman, so now she is a Hun."

Attila is struggling with what he is hearing. "Sometimes, you are very, very strange!"

"I want her," said Zehun, feeling he is finally on solid ground. "She is special."

Attila shook his head and sighed deeply. "Okay. You're a great fighter, so you can have what you want. I just do not understand. You can have any woman under the sun, because you are my lieutenant, and … you want *this* one! Sometimes I think you see the dust, not the storm."

After a while, Attila said in a different tone, "We would have killed a lot more Romans if our horses hadn't given out. Romans are good with their short swords, but we are better with arrows. We have to change our way of fighting."

"The horses were exhausted," Bleda said. "A year of constant fighting – a long time."

"We should rest them before each battle," added Zehun.

Attila pondered this while he sat now on a narrow log and watched the Danube flow by. He shifted his position and sat on a flat rock, seeking more comfort. And then he was struck by a powerful revelation. His horses gave out because the weight of the rider was bearing on a concentrated area of the back. His own backside had hurt when all his weight was pressed onto a narrow log, but now the comfort was greater when he spread it over a large area of a flat rock. How stupid of him not to have realized this before! Inspired, he fashioned two planks, much longer than the stiff under panels of the saddle originally invented by the Sarmatians. He strapped them on his horse and mounted.

Bleda and his assistants were highly amused. They thought Attila had gone mad, until they noticed that Attila's horse did not drop its back, despite being tender. The horse did not lift its head, as horses will do when a sore back is pressed. Bleda stopped laughing when Attila stood on the planks and jumped up and down with his weight. All went well until one of the planks shifted; Attila lost his balance and fell ignominiously on his rear end. A roar of laughter went up from the spectators. Attila paid no attention. He was looking at the planks and the horse was looking at him, and they shared a picture of comfort.

"And one more thing," said Attila. "We need to stand to launch spears and fire arrows. It will make us more stable! I have seen an old foot platform used by the Chinese."

So Attila went to work. He fashioned a wooden plank half the length of his boot and wide enough to clear both sides, and then hung it from his "new" saddle with strips of leather. He climbed aboard and now, for the first time, stood in the stirrups.

Attila asked Zehun for his bow, stood in the stirrups, and at the trot, fired an arrow at a bean curd he had asked to be hung from a tree fifty yards away. It struck dead center.

Over the next two days, Attila tried various methods of keeping the extended planks and affixed wooden stirrups in place. Finally what worked was the arch formed naturally when mangroves reached down into the estuaries of the Danube, making a natural right angle. The wood was incredibly strong. Using wet horsehide, he secured the arches to the planks. When the rawhide shrank it contracted, making a bond of great strength. Then he slung more hide between the arches, let it dry for three days ... and a much stronger version of the original Sarmatian wood frame was born. Forever after in history, the solid part of a saddle would be called a "tree," because Attila first used an actual mangrove tree to replace the old wooden frame.

Attila rode the horse for days, making multiple corrections, listening always to the horse for advice. The horse was telling him everything was fine – no back pain. Attila stood now, put an arrow in his bow, turned toward camp, and at full gallop, standing in the stirrups, he put a second arrow in the bean curd still hanging from a tree. Bleda was shocked. He knew Attila was good with the bow, but he never thought he was that good!

"Great," yelled Zehun.

Attila turned, rode back, dismounted, and told Bleda and Zehun, "It is the beginning of a new day for the Huns. We will make new saddles with stirrups cast in bronze."

Bleda bowed his head in respect, his silence an acknowledgment of the superior powers of his brother.

Attila turned to Zehun. "As you seem to have problems raping villagers, I will put you in charge of saddle production. Make slaves out of the vermin. You don't have to rape them! They can't make saddles if they're dead. So no need to kill them!" He laughed heartily, which is something he almost never did. He knew life was about to change.

For a year, the Huns set about building saddles and casting bronze stirrups. Everything grew better in design as the warriors and their enslaved workers became more skilled. All this time, the horses were resting and grazing on good spring grass.

So with fresh mounts, solid saddles, rested men, restrung bows and sharpened weapons, Attila and Bleda moved north, plundering villages and settlements as they went. Attila was pleased with the success of his stirrups and saddles. His men quickly learned how to stand and fire their arrows. The backs of the horses stayed strong. Because there was little resistance, Attila allowed his men to enjoy the spoils. They ate, drank, and raped. And then they moved on, sacking the walled city of Margus with the help of a captured bishop, who secured his own life by opening the gates. It was here that Attila was joined by another hoard of Saracen horsemen, who saw great gain in joining a superior force. Still other Huns arrived, having fled the ranks of Roman armies that had conscripted them. The men enjoyed the freedom Attila gave them. All they had to do was kill on command. Raping was a bonus. The Romans had so much discipline, so many rules; the new warriors liked Attila's easy style.

Finally, Attila was facing the walls of a prize of his dreams – the city of Constantinople. He was met by a strong force of Roman foot soldiers and horse archers, led by Romanized German generals. It was here Attila first used a tactic he would employ for the rest of his days. He fled, as if in retreat, and the Romans took the bait. They galloped after him, following Attila into a large flat valley, with hills sloping up on either side. Three days later, the column of bareback Romans was spread over three miles, as their horses slowed in various stages of exhaustion, their backs spent. A day earlier, Attila had dispatched a squadron of warriors to return back to the start of the valley, using low-lying trees on far sides of the valley as cover and moving only at night. They would effectively stop any retreat by the Romans. The Huns were still way in front of the charge, out of range of the Roman archers. Attila galloped up to higher ground and looked back down the valley, and was pleased to see most of the Romans were now on foot, their horses finished. They were assembling in battle formation. This amused Attila. There were no Huns in front of them to fight! Attila was pleased that he would not have to fight the Romans hand to hand, because they were masterful with their short swords, always managing to get under the arc of a circling Hun axe or heavy broadsword. Attila would now fight the Romans on his terms.

Midafternoon of the third day, the Huns formed ranks on higher ground, dismounted, and filled the sky with arrows. The bows were the finest in the medieval world, with a killing range of three hundred yards – more powerful than Roman bows. (The English longbow, then in development, would never exceed a killing range of two hundred yards.) On that day, over one thousand Roman soldiers were dead or dying in the setting sun. Attila gave orders not to purposely shoot horses, as they could be useful. On the morning of the next day, another two thousand Romans died, some shot in the chest by the warriors Attila had placed at the valley exit. Others were shot in the back, while they tried desperately to flee the trap. Attila spared the life of the leading general only so he could go back to his emperor with the message: send two thousand pounds of gold annually, or Constantinople would be attacked. He would send much of this gold to Zehun to pay villagers for saddle production. The gold encouraged greater effort.

Attila ordered his men to go over the fields littered with dead and dying Romans. The wounded were speared. The Huns pulled out bloody arrows, cleaned them, and returned them to quivers. Roman soldiers who were alive and in good shape were stripped of their armor and their ankles fitted with rawhide hobbles. Attila would use them as pack animals to save his horses. The Romans would march until they dropped, and then they would be speared. This soon became standard after-battle procedure.

Word of the success spread to other factions of the Huns, who came to join forces and bestow upon Attila the title King of the Huns. Attila claimed he was in possession of the Sword of Mars, handed to him by a peasant, he said, and that this gave him direct communication with the God of War. In the winter of 445, Attila commanded over 100,000 men, and about then he decided there could be only one King of the Huns, so he murdered his brother, Bleda. He liked Bleda, but he liked exclusive power more. Attila's ranks were filling now not just with Huns, but with anybody who wanted to enjoy the spoils of plunder. There were Romans and Greeks, Turks and Persians, Germans and others from an ancient land once called Sarmatia. He taught them how to ride like a true Hun and kill like a Hun and delight in letting blood. He showed them the joys of plunder and looting and raping. His only code of moral conduct was: be kind to your horse. He let his warriors know all the world was theirs to enjoy – all other people were merely caretakers. Every living creature was the property of the Huns, laid at their feet on command from the God of War. Most of all, Attila taught them how to care for and respect horses, and to communicate in the old way. Mistreating a horse was punishable by death. He called his horses "chariots of the Gods," and he put their worth and moral value above that of any other creature or any human being. There was no way back from mistreating or disrespecting a horse.

When Roman senators came to appease Attila – bearing gifts as always – he would not speak to them unless he was seated on a horse and they were seated on the ground. Often the decisions he made were "prompted" by the horse. In these "conversations" with his horse, he was notorious for demanding there be no interruptions. Assistants were slain on a regular basis, always by Attila's own hand, because they sneezed or otherwise caused a distraction during these man-and-horse conferences.

Flush with tribute gold from the Romans, which would continue on a yearly basis, Attila was able to finance even more massive expansion in weapons. Whole villages were enslaved in the manufacture of saddlery, under the direction of Zehun. To keep his men battle fit and to satisfy their lust for blood, Attila encouraged them to roam and plunder freely. For Attila, killing was not a means to grab property. Indeed, he never colonized any of the great number of countries he conquered. He simply killed and destroyed and moved on. For Attila, killing was reward unto itself.

Attila liked the idea of extracting a ton of gold annually from the Romans simply by not attacking them. And he kept his deal. If they didn't pay him on time, he would attack some Roman-occupied city of note. If they paid up, he would amuse himself by attacking non-Roman territories. He was careful never to let his men lose their lust for blood.

Feeling empowered by the God of War – and somewhat bored, Attila in 447 launched a massive attack on Constantinople; again, the Romans were a little late on their annual payment. But as the Huns bore down on the city, *a catastrophic earthquake struck.* Of course, the earthquake was attributed to Attila's supernatural powers, a fact that he himself believed after the by-chance natural disaster. The ground shook with the thunder of 100,000 horses, and buildings were swallowed by the convoluting earth. The Romans went to the defense of the city, but again they lost. They had little will to fight, convinced that Attila could indeed invoke the gods. They were awed by his power and his brutality, and they fled his wrath as best they could. More took an arrow in the back than the chest.

At the end of the fighting, Attila and his lieutenants sat on their horses and observed the incredible destruction before them.

"A magnificent sight," said Attila.

"More dead Romans," said a lieutenant. "This is good. Romans colonize people and bend them to the Roman ways. They deserve to die."

"So," said another lieutenant, "we just kill! Is there a difference? Would slaves rather be dead?"

"Don't know," said Attila. "I've never been a slave, and I've never been dead."

The lieutenants chuckled respectfully.

"We do not enslave them. We just kill them," continued Attila. "So they call us barbarians. But the Romans, they are the barbarians. They conquer and enslave. We, the Huns, we do not colonize. We take what we want and move on. And we, the Huns, are the better warriors. Witness now!"

The words hung there for a beat, and then Attila added, "I have observed the Romans do not fight as well running backward as they do running forward."

Attila owned the Balkans. But once again, Attila had no interest in annexing Constantinople. Better to let the Romans rebuild the city, and then he would attack again, and occupy a city beautifully rebuilt!

As history would have it, Attila was striking the Romans when they were at their weakest. Their empire was crumbling due to a long run of economic failures, along with heavy troop costs on the Persian front.

The Huns were not building empires. They were tearing them down. They lusted for the sport of plunder and delighted in striking fear and loathing.

Attila relished his new title in the civilized world – the Scourge of God.

Sometime in 450, Attila turned his focus to the West. He thought if he could unseat the Roman-Barbarian Aetius by marching with the Western Emperor Valentinian and ridding Roman landowners of the Visigoths, he could become Emperor of the West, with permission from Rome. In his quest to become "respectable," Attila tried to marry Valentinian's sister. She told him what he did not want to hear: that he was a barbarian, a savage, with no worthwhile human values. She ordered him to vacate her space. For Attila, nothing was working in the "civilized" world. He told himself he didn't much like being "civilized" anyhow. So once more, Attila assembled his forces, crossed the Rhine, and battled a formidable force of Gallic and Frank soldiers. Aetius and Attila finally squared off somewhere in Champagne in June 451 in a battle so fierce historians would later describe it as Armageddon. For the first time in a decade, Attila was forced to retreat. The Visigoths had the upper hand.

Attila and his battered forces escaped into Italy. It was here he learned of an attack on his home territory by Eastern Empire forces, so he rushed back to what would become Hungary. His plan was to assemble another massive army, and finally, one more time, seize and this time *keep* Constantinople while it was being rebuilt. This act, he was convinced, would once again generate mule trains of gold from the Romans. Not that he needed money. He never paid for anything anyhow, except the arms and saddlery production managed by Zehun, who had "this problem" with killing the defenseless. Otherwise, Attila just took what he wanted. But he loved the idea of extracting gold from the Romans and seeing what pain and sacrifice that caused them. He passed on the gold to his followers, having no need for it himself. Gold and plunder consolidated loyalty. During a ten-year period, the Romans were sending him, on average, a ton of gold annually. If he couldn't marry into the Roman power structure, he now decided, he would take the whole Roman Empire and make it his own. He would change his policy in future. He would attack, capture – and hold. He had visions of how he would deal with Valentinian's sister. Now that would be fun! Oh yes, she would gladly marry him after he was done with her.

He was feeling so good about this plan he decided to take another wife. He threw a great party, got very drunk (something he did rarely), and passed out. During the night, he choked to death on a nosebleed. The year was 453. He was forty-seven years old – ancient for a fighting man at that time. In twenty-five years of power, Attila was defeated only once. His new wife was buried with him. She was fifteen years old. She died a virgin.

CHAPTER NINETEEN

Emma is devastated upon learning Tower has been sold. The earth has been pulled from under her. She feels betrayed, bewildered, shocked. How could they do this! She locks herself in her room. She comes out only for meals, and then she sits sullen at the table. She does not respond to attempts at conversation. Meanwhile, news from school is mixed. She is getting into trouble, but is "socializing." Clearly, just weeks into the medication, she has changed. She was sent home from school when a teacher found her interacting "inappropriately" with two young men.

Allan is pleased his daughter is now becoming more "normal," but Millie is not happy. She calls the parents of the boys involved. They promise reprimand.

* * *

Saturday, May 29. Emma stands in the hallway outside her bedroom and confronts her mother.

"I don't feel well," she says. "I feel … strange."

Millie takes her in her arms, expecting her to step away from this kind of contact. To her surprise, Emma does not back off. Millie brushes her hair. Still Emma does not object. "You're going to be all right," says Millie softly.

Next morning, at breakfast, Emma looks at the "vitamins" set out as usual by her orange juice. She looks at them for a long time. When Millie has her back turned, Emma puts them in her jeans pocket.

"We have no horses," says Emma.

Millie comes to her side and puts her arm around her. Again, no flinching from the personal contact, Millie notes, and she asks herself if this is good, or bad. Does Emma feel her holding her, or does she feel nothing? Millie ponders this, then dismisses further inward discussion and adds, "We can't afford horses. I know you miss Tower." And then she takes a step back, holds Emma at arm's length, and says, excited, "Tell you what: I'll take you to Suzanne's, and you can ride one of her mules. What about that?"

Emma nods. "Whatever."

* * *

Later that morning, while Emma is visiting Suzanne and Jules, Millie leaves the kitchen of her home and goes down the path and into the well pump room, where Allan is working on a faulty switch.

"We have to talk," she says.

"Yeah, I figured." Allan puts down a socket wrench. "Look," he says, "I know we haven't been getting along lately – a lot of stress. And I know there is something going on with you. I didn't want to say anything, but I called back that number that was on your cell phone and I was surprised to hear an English voice that I recognize."

Millie looks stunned. "You're … you're monitoring my phone!"

"Couldn't help it. I just wanted to know, you know, give myself some warning."

Millie is silent a while and then she says, a tone of confession in her voice, "I should have told you. That was Harry back in town. He is auditioning for a big part in a new television series, and he just wanted to see how I was doing."

For a very long time Allen looks at her, and then he says, "Why didn't you tell me?"

"I ... didn't think it was necessary."

Again, a long pause. Allan looks at her steadily. "Is anything going on here that I should be concerned about?"

"No," says Millie, more sternly now. "Nothing is going on!"

"Okay, okay."

The two stand in silence, the hum of an electric motor the only sound.

"You know," says Allan quietly, "I love you, and I don't want all this to go away."

"It's not going away," Millie says.

Allan says, "Well, at least we have each other, as they say."

Now Millie rolls her eyes. "Yeah, great consolation prize!"

Allan looks at his feet, and for a moment looks like he is going to say something.

But it is Millie who steps toward him, puts a hand on each of his shoulders, and says, "I'm sorry; I didn't mean that. Allan, I love you."

For a long while, they hold each other.

Then Allan reassures, "We're going to get through this."

"Yes, we will," says Millie, and she feels hot tears running down her face.

Allan squeezes her tight.

Millie steps back, takes a deep breath, and then wipes her tears away and kind of laughs. "This – what we've been talking about – this is not why I came into the pump room."

Allan looks surprised.

"What I came to talk to you about is Emma. She is acting really strange, and I know it is that medication."

"People acting strange is the order of the day around here!"

"Yeah, well, that aside, I do not like the way Emma is behaving," says Millie.

"Look, she was strange before. Now she is, well, like a normal teenager, all screwed up. But I could do without the boys at this time."

"Well," says Millie, "now you've got normal. And making out with boys is normal!"

"So her interests are broadening. She's becoming … more … social," adds Allan.

"But … but she's lost interest in horses. And she's getting into trouble at school. Unruly, they're calling it. Where's all this going?"

"Getting into trouble is what teenage girls do. Now that is normal!" Allan says flatly.

A silence falls between them as they leave the pump room and head on up to the den. Allan hits the remote. They sit, sighing simultaneously. There is a news special, but they are not watching. They are using the television as cover for no conversation.

That afternoon, Emma goes to her room and shuts the door. She does not come out for dinner.

"Leave her be," says Millie, anticipating a remark from Allan.

Later, as they lie in bed that night, Millie says, "I … miss the Emma we used to know. I am having trouble understanding this Emma. I'm … I'm afraid for her."

"She's a lot more normal than she used to be is all I can say," Allan offers.

"I don't know if normal is good."

"She was going to kill herself on that horse," says Allan.

"I don't think so. I never saw her in danger on Tower."

"That's not what Manuel told me on Monday."

Millie looks at him and frowns.

"I never told you," continues Allan, "didn't want to worry you, but she came off on a jump."

Now Millie sits upright in bed. "You should have told me!"

"I figured you had enough on your plate, one way or another."

Millie sighs, then says, "You broke her heart when you sold Tower."

"I probably saved her life. Anyway, we needed the money. We saved the ranch."

"We could have found the money some other place."

"You know that's not true."

Silence, and then Millie says, "Yeah, I know."

Millie's tone levels with deliberation. "I don't care what happens, we are taking Emma off that medication. I want our daughter back, the way she was born."

"We'll have to talk with Dr. Rosenthal about that."

Down the hall, Emma lies awake in bed. For weeks now, she's had no visions, has not gone to that place far away and long ago. She has looked at her lithographs, and they have done nothing for her. She feels confused, frustrated. Her life, she concludes, has become very stressful. Will she ever see Zehun again?

CHAPTER TWENTY

Sunday, June 20. It is a beautiful early summer day at the Santa Barbara Showgrounds, and Earl Holloway and his wife, Jennifer, a plump and pleasant woman, are joined by a dozen of their wealthy friends. They have ringside seats in the main arena. Earl is a sponsor. The event is a feature of the Summer Classics. The division is amateur hunters over fences. Champagne flutes are served by liveried waiters. Cute girls in tuxedo shirts offer hors-d'oeuvres – bacon rolls, pineapple slices, coconut shrimp.

Earl fires a giant cigar and announces, "Thanks, my friends, for gracing me with your presence." He sips his champagne, glowing in the moment, and continues, "I was going to take Tower over these fences myself. It is, after all, Father's Day, and I could pull rank. But I thought I'd give Mary the honors."

Laughter bursts at the collective vision of Earl going over anything more physically dangerous than a profit-and-loss sheet.

"There are," boasts Earl, "some fine horses entered, but I'll take bets at ten-to-one that Mary and Tower will get the blue."

Glasses clink. Hands find wallets. Bets are on.

The announcer requests contestants run in the order in which they have been pulled from a hat. There are words of thanks to Earl for his generous patronage and support. Applause ripples around the perfectly groomed arena. Earl stands, bows.

The first horse, a warmblood, easily clears the fences. As does a stunning gray Arabian/Parkbred. Now Mary is at the starting gate, and the arena officer indicates *go*. Mary's short, stout size makes Tower look even bigger than his seventeen hands. A great round of applause as Tower moves off to the first jump. No problems there. He clears the second jump, but there was a moment of hesitation, as if Tower is distracted. Mary is a picture of concentration as she approaches the third jump. She gives Tower a sharp whack on the rump with her crop, and his head snaps up. Tower is not happy being hit, not happy with the unsteady weight of this rider on his back. He looks confused, but he will do the best he can. He is sending pictures, but there is no response. He is not receiving pictures either. All he can do is take charge. He knows, now, he is alone. Tower increases both his speed and his stride as he approaches the jump, but he looks to where Mary is looking – *at* the jump. Instead of going over, he plants his front hooves deep into the plowed earth, to take an even closer look at the jump. He is looking to where Mary was looking. In his peripheral vision, he had seen Mary concentrating on the jump – not at a point beyond, so he did what he thought she wanted him to do – stop at the jump she was looking at. In an instant, Mary is launched out of the saddle, making a perfect arc over the red, white, and blue poles. She lands flat on her back. She does not move. The poles are untouched.

Earl is on his feet, face frozen in fear and disbelief. Spectators gasp as one. Earl is climbing the fence now and running across the arena, shedding en route both champagne glass and cigar. He drops to Mary's side and screams, "Medics! We need a doctor *now*!" And within seconds, paramedics are pushing him aside, and an ambulance is speeding onto the field, sirens blaring, lights flashing. Fifteen minutes later, the whirl of a helicopter.

"She's going to be all right," says a white-robed attendant as he tries tactfully to move Earl to one side.

"Her eyes are closed!" Earl screams.

"But she's breathing," says the attendant.

The arena is cleared, and the helicopter lands by the jumps. Mary is loaded aboard. Earl begs to go with her. There is resistance, but finally they let him aboard and the chopper lifts, circles and heads south.

In the north corner of the arena, a ring assistant has caught Tower and is leading him out, back toward the barns.

* * *

Sunday night, at Cedars Sinai Hospital, Earl learns Mary has a broken collarbone, a broken right wrist, a concussion, and – doctors suspect – two cracked ribs. Had she not been wearing a helmet, the senior staff physician tells Earl, she might not have survived.

Mary's mother, Jennifer, and three friends have driven from Santa Barbara. They are gathered now in a room adjoining Mary's urgent care ward. The mood is grim. A doctor offers reassuring views on the various injuries. "At this point," he says carefully, "there's nothing that appears to be life-threatening."

* * *

Meanwhile, back at Earl's ranch in Sherman Oaks, Tower has been put in an isolated stall. It is approaching midnight now, and the head trainer, Lewis Williams, an Englishman who claimed to have worked at the Royal Stables in London, is leaning on the half-door and looking at Tower.

Lewis Williams has thickened a little since his steeplechase days. He is of medium height, balding, with a goatee beard, an adornment that makes him appealing for walk-through parts in Western or period movies. He nurses a brandy toddy, as is his style, and studies Tower. At Earl's instruction, he has never jumped the horse, just exercised it. Earl had told him glowing reports of Tower's ability over fences, so Earl assumed the horse was a great jumper. Why, he asks himself now, had Tower refused a fence at Santa Barbara? "Recalcitrant," he says to himself. The horse was simply being defiant. Tomorrow, he decides, he would give him an "attitude adjustment."

Williams takes a swig from his toddy, and says to Tower, "We're gonna get on this tomorrow."

CHAPTER TWENTY-ONE

Monday, June 21. Dawn breaks on Earl Holloway's estate, and Lewis Williams has saddled Tower and is riding him in the main exercise arena. Earl and Jennifer have remained at Cedars Sinai with Mary, who is still in "guarded" condition.

"Okay," says Williams to Tower, "now today's lesson is ... Who is the Boss?" Williams is alone, except for a Mexican day worker taking instructions on where to put the jump poles. Williams starts Tower over a series of cavaletties – poles laid on the ground, one pace apart – and trots him through those to a "bounce" jump at the end. The jump is set at two feet. The idea is to get the horse to "pace" himself as he approaches the jump, and is thus set up for a good takeoff. Several times, Williams takes Tower through the exercise, and each time it is perfect. The jump is raised to three feet. Again, perfect. Now the jump is raised to four feet, and the pole nearest the jump is moved back two paces, giving the horse more takeoff room. This time, even before he enters Tower into the line of cavaletties, Williams lays the crop heavily on Tower's rump and then sinks rowel spurs deep into his side. Tower jumps with the sudden pain and rushes the cavaletties, scattering the one nearest the jump, but still has enough momentum to go forward and, with one mighty leap, manages to clear the collapsing jump, executing an impossible spread of ground between takeoff and landing. Williams ends up on Tower's neck, but stays aboard. Turning out of the jump, he whips Tower in a fit of rage, yelling and cursing. "We're gonna do better than that, you rotten bastard!"

Tower's eyes are wide with fear as he approaches a second similar jump. Again, he hits the top pole. All the while, Williams is whipping and spurring and cursing. Tower clears the poles still in place, takes an extra long stride to clear the pole knocked to the ground, stumbles, regains his balance, and then *explodes*, bucking on all fours, then rearing, then dropping his head and firing up his massive rear end. Williams is launched high in the air and comes down on his head. He tries to sit up, but then falls back. The Mexican worker rushes to him, sees there is blood frothing up from his mouth, and then runs back up to the big house, where Rosetta, the maid, calls 911. Paramedics arrive within twenty minutes, make an evaluation, and request a helicopter. Within fifty minutes, Lewis Williams is on the same floor in the same hospital as Mary Holloway. When Williams can focus, the first person he sees is Earl, standing like cast stone at the end of his bed. Earl barks, "What the hell happened?"

Williams tries to explain, but cannot. He fades into a soft, deep, dark, drug-induced sleep.

With Mary now off the "guarded" list and resting comfortably, Earl leaves the hospital at midnight Monday and returns home. He does not drive up into the carport. Instead, he stops at the stables, finds Tower, halters him to an iron ring bolted into the concrete wall, and produces a cattle prod. "Now, you son of a bitch, for all the hurt you've caused me, here is some for you." And he shocks the horse unmercifully. Tower screams, rears, and snaps the brass clip on the halter. He falls back and smashes his head against the steel stable door. Then he is very still, legs twitching. Earl hits him again with the cattle prod, but Tower is knocked out, cold. With each electric shock he twitches, then goes still.

"Good," says Earl, snarling, "You did it to yourself. I hope you never wake up!"

He slams the stable door, returns the red-handled cattle prod, and drives on up to the big house, tires squealing on the blacktop.

* * *

While Mary had been riding Tower at Santa Barbara on Sunday and crashing, Jules and Emma were sitting by the waterfall, where they always meet, high in the Santa Monica Mountains. The sun is dropping lower in the sky. They have ridden here on mules from Jules's ranch.

Jules has brought sandwiches, two cans of soda, and once again, his history book.

They snuggle close. Emma feels the warmth of his body invade her whole being.

"Read to me, please."

"Okay," and Jules smiles broadly.

"You say it, makes it real."

"It *is* real. Just time has shifted." He looks over at Rocket and Sundance. "Now those mules haven't changed. They're still the same as they were hundreds of thousands of years. Just different. Bigger maybe."

"You know what doctors said, I have brain like … the same as a horse's brain. Very old, he says."

Jules looks at her and frowns. "Now that is, like, weird."

"Says you have that brain too. Everybody does. But not everybody uses it."

"I have that brain?"

"Yes. Doctor said. He gave me something to stop me using this brain. Mother said they were vitamins."

Jules stares at her for a long moment, and then shakes his head. "Vitamins wouldn't do that! They're giving you something else …"

Emma is silent. She wants to speak, but no words come.

Jules nods, as if something has just been revealed. "Well, that explains it. That's why the way you talk is changing. You just made a complete correct sentence."

"How am I different?"

"You don't sound like a tape recorder anymore. Well, not always."

"Is that good?"

"I don't know …"

Silence, and then Jules adds, "You're different now."

"I *feel* different. I don't feel good. I just feel … different."

There is silence for a short while, then Emma sighs, as if she has made some big decision. "I want to show you something," she says, reaching into the pocket of her coat. She pulls out a white plastic bottle, hands it to Jules. "This is what I have been taking."

Jules studies the label carefully. "Naltrexone. Okay. I'm going to research this at the library. Doesn't look like vitamins to me! I got my own computer at work, did I tell you that?"

"Good," says Emma, "something is not right here." She looks at Rocket and Sundance. They are dozing standing. There are no pictures.

Jules looks at the mules too. He turns to Emma. "Something here has *really* changed, and I don't like it. You are sounding like everybody else. It's not *you*."

"I know," says Emma. "I don't like it either."

Jules opens the book. "You'll love this. It was one of your favorite chapters. This is where Attila improves the saddle invented way before by the Sarmatians, and copies an old stirrup from the Chinese. This changed everything!" Jules is excited now, and his speech becomes more rapid. "Attila lets the Romans chase him, and their horses wear out, and then they must dismount, but Attila still has horses, so he has set the trap, and he gains high ground and just kills them all, with his arrows." He punches the book with his finger. "It says here 'the arrows fell like rain.' Attila was very glad he had found a way not to have to fight the Romans man-to-man. The Romans were the best with that short sword. Now isn't that *way* cool!"

"Yes," says Emma. "Attila put Zehun in charge of making the saddles. He told the villagers he would guarantee their safety if they worked for him."

Jules looks at Emma and frowns, then asks, "Where did you get that? And where did you get that name, Zehun?"

"I don't know. You must have read it to me."

"Well, Zehun was a common name in the time of Attila. And Attila had many lieutenants. But I do not ever remember mentioning to you the name Zehun."

After a while, Emma looks down and says very quietly, "There's something I must tell you …"

"Yes …"

"I get visions. Until now. Always had them, about places far away and long ago. They are so real, so… *there*. Always, I meet Zehun, and somehow I am always involved with him. He never wants to hurt me. He always trying to save me."

"Well," says Jules, "sounds to me like nice dreams."

"But … but I love him."

"They are dreams, something in your mind."

"No, no. You don't understand. They are *not* dreams. It is like I am transported to another place." She looks straight at Jules now and asks, "Do you dream?"

"Why, yes, sometimes."

"Do you remember, the dream?"

"Maybe, for about two seconds after I wake."

"Well," says Emma, looking straight into his eyes, this time with more penetration than before, "I remember *everything*. The smell of the horses in those villages, and how that smell is different from the smell of my own horses. I smell the smoke from the village fires. I hear the screams of people dying as they are being attacked by the Huns, swords and spears cutting into their bodies. But ... but I can't get there anymore."

Jules's eyes widen. "That's intense."

"And Zehun looks *exactly* like you."

Jules sighs heavily. "Well, that's very nice, but I am not Zehun. That would make me about sixteen hundred years old. I know I'm getting older, but I'm not *that* old!"

Emma laughs and shakes her head. "You must think I'm weird."

Jules cups her head in his massive, strong hands and says, "I think you are the most beautiful girl I have ever known in my life. You are the most beautiful girl I could ever imagine."

Emma blushes, lowers her eyes, and says nothing.

Then Jules laughs and says, "I'm not surprised Zehun has the hots for you! He's no fool!"

For a long time, they listen to the waterfall, and then Emma says, "Attila was cruel."

"That was war. Either the Romans died, or Attila died. That's what they did back then," says Jules. Then he smiles cheekily and adds, "You should know. You go back there often. Or at least you did."

"I was *taken* there. But then … I haven't been back there since they put me on that medication. It's like the entrance is closed to this place where I like to go, where I find comfort – it's like … I'm not free now."

Jules looks at her. "There you go. More complete sentences! Anyhow, do you like … going back there?"

"I did. It was very violent. I just don't understand all the killing, the pain. Still, it's just strange not to be going back."

Jules absentmindedly flips the pages in his book, and then he says, "War is still happening today. People are being killed every day in Afghanistan, and a lot of them are innocents, women and children, unarmed peasants. They are dying just as they were when Genghis Khan rode through the same land. Nothing has changed. It's what people do – kill each other."

"Why is that?"

"I don't know. I don't think anybody knows. If they did, they would stop killing each other, because it's a no-win deal. To kill somebody is a lot of work. It must make you feel bad. And … to be killed, well, that would be worse!"

Emma looks at his book and says, "Read the part where Attila wants to marry the sister of the Roman governor of Constantinople, but she kicks him out of the palace because she says he is a savage. I think he really loved her, and that is sad, that they never, well, married each other ... she might have tamed him."

"No way! Attila could never be tamed."

Jules turns now to Emma and says, "Hey, before I get into this, tell me, does Zehun have a girlfriend in your visions?"

For an instant, Emma is startled, then confused. "I ... I never thought about that. But then, he acts like I am his girlfriend."

Jules rocks back his head and laughs. "I'm sure glad he's not real."

Jules looks back at his book, to change the subject. But before he can proceed, Emma says, "Did you hear what I said? I think he thinks I am his girlfriend!"

Jules looks at her and smiles. "All I can say is Zehun has great taste!"

Emma smiles uncertainly and settles back, her head on Jules's shoulder as he begins to read, moving through Attila's attempt to get respectable by trying to marry into Roman power, then to where Attila decided to do things the way he always did, with brute force:

> ... the year was 447, and Attila launched a massive attack on Constantinople. *At the same time, a massive earthquake struck.* Of course, the earthquake was attributed to Attila's supernatural powers, a fact he himself believed after the by-chance earthquake. The ground shook with the thunder of 100,000 horses as

Romans fell screaming and buildings collapsed in rubble and …

Emma sees all this as her consciousness drifts off into a familiar place. For just an instant, she sees Zehun there now, being attacked by a dozen Romans bearing down on him. He charges at them, first letting fly three precisely placed arrows, and now he is upon the Romans. He jumps off his horse, sword swinging, and the Romans close in, but they are no match for Zehun. He screams and swings his sword, and in the light of burning buildings, there is blood everywhere, and the air is filled with screams and …

Next thing Emma knows, Jules is shaking her, and she sees Jules looking down at her now. She hears the gentle gurgle of the waterfall. She looks over and sees the mules. The points of reference snap her back to the present. She looks up at Jules, who is more concerned than she has ever seen. "Are you all right?" he asks urgently. "You must have been having a nightmare."

"No, I saw you. I mean, I saw Zehun! It was for just an instant. But I went back."

Jules rolls his eyes. "Not him again!"

Emma looks at Jules and takes a deep breath. "He is a great warrior. Attila likes him. But most of Attila's other leaders distrust Zehun because he doesn't like to see women and children killed. He likes only to kill Romans. They are armed and he is armed, but he is better than they are. He likes that."

Jules laughs, shakes the mood, and says, "Hey, I'm starting to like this dude."

There is a silence between them, and then Jules asks, "Now, are you okay?"

Emma looks up at him, and her whole body is consumed with a warm, soft pleasure. "Oh, yeah," she says, smiling and relaxing now with a deep breath. "I'm better than all right!"

CHAPTER TWENTY-TWO

Tuesday, June 22. A friend texts Emma about Mary's crash at Santa Barbara on Sunday, while Emma had been at the waterfall with Jules. Her heart sinks as she feels for Tower and how he was being ridden and what he was going through. And then she feels guilt for worrying more about Tower than about Mary.

At dinner, Emma brings up the subject of Mary's crash. Allan explains what happened, how Tower stopped at a jump, launching Mary.

"We just heard about it today," says Millie.

Silence, except for the scrape of silverware on plates.

Allan and Millie exchange glances, then Allan says, "Mary is not much of a rider anyhow."

Suddenly, Emma speaks. "Mary didn't show pictures of him jumping, not like I used to."

Allan and Millie look at each other, and then Allan says, "You said … *used* to."

"Yes. I don't see pictures anymore," Emma says matter-of-factly.

Millie is silent a while, and then announces, "That's it. We're taking you off the vitamins."

Emma drops her fork with a clatter. "They're not vitamins, Mother. It's medication. To do something with my brain."

Millie and Allan look at each other, failing to hide their shock.

"Hey," says Allan quickly, "whatever, it is to help you."

Emma looks down at her plate, then she sits upright, resolve in her posture. "Doesn't matter anyhow. I stopped taking them a couple of weeks ago. I want to be myself."

Allan takes in a sudden gulp of air, and Millie cuts him a glance. After a while Allan says, "Look, Emma, you shouldn't be making decisions like that. We're here to help you."

"I don't need help. Need Tower."

"Now look here," says Allan, "we'll get you another damn horse! The reason we have no horses is because we can't afford them and we have to sell the property."

"Okay. Okay!" Millie interjects, taking note with some relief that Emma seems to be going back to her old speech pattern. "We've been over this page before."

Suddenly Allan stands, takes his plate to the sink, and leaves.

"No horses," says Emma, calling after him.

Millie puts an arm around Emma. "We will get through this. I know you miss Tower."

Emma is blinking rapidly now. "What ... where Tower? What happened after the crash?"

"I don't know," says Allan, turning and standing in the doorway. He knew, of course. Earl had called him, wanting his money back. Allan had told him he didn't have any money to do a refund on Tower, and Earl had told him, "Fine. This horse is outta here. He's a killer. My daughter and the trainer are in hospital *at the same time!*" And he had slammed down the phone.

Another silence, and then Millie says, "For a special treat, Emma, I am going to take you someplace you'll like this weekend."

Emma leaves the kitchen. Millie goes down the hall and follows Allan into their bedroom. She shuts the door. "I feel bad for lying about the medication. I should have been honest."

Allan rolls his eyes. "Look, I don't care about that. We're putting her back on that medication. That was making her normal. We can't fail her."

"The only person who has failed here is you. We are broke because you can't train a horse to run. You could at least get a paying job somewhere. You have destroyed Emma by selling Tower."

"Emma will be better off normal. We've got to get her back on the medication!"

"No, we are not!" Millie snaps. "Not ever – not *ever!*"

* * *

Emma goes to her room, locks the door, pulls out her lithographs, drinks in the pictures, closes her eyes, and now she is *wanting* to go back. She feels it coming, and she is ready. She puts away the lithographs, throws herself on the bed, and feels the darkness rushing toward her in that familiar pattern. She is *so* relieved she is feeling like her old self!

She hears water flowing, and for an instant Emma thinks she is back at the waterfall with Jules. But then she realizes she is dressed in deerskin, and she knows she is back in that place, long ago and far away. A woven basket is over her arm. She has been collecting berries. Her sword and bow are at her side. She plucks a berry from the basket and tastes it. The particular sweetness is something she has never experienced. She is thinking about this when she hears a noise behind her, and she turns, alarmed. She grabs her sword, stands, and is ready to strike. Then, she lowers it and is flooded with relief. Standing there is Zehun. He is also wearing deerskin, from his head to feet that are strapped with high fur boots. The hilt of his sword protrudes from under the deer hide around his waist.

"I'm sorry if I startled you," says Zehun.

He sits beside her, and Emma moves quickly away. "I'm not going to hurt you. I've been looking for you," he says, and then looks at her sword. "I am happy to see you are now armed, at least!"

Emma relaxes, but says nothing.

"Sorry your village was attacked, this time by the Romans."

"It wasn't my village. I was only visiting."

"Where is your family?"

"I don't know. Maybe dead. They probably think I have been killed."

Zehun puts his hand on her shoulder. "I am here to take care of you, as I promised."

Emma looks at the berries in her basket. The hand on the hilt of the sword relaxes.

"What ... what are you doing back here?" Emma asks.

"I've come for you. It is not safe here for you anymore. More Romans are coming from the south. Many legions. They want to occupy all the area to the steppes."

Zehun reaches into her basket and takes out a handful of berries. "So," he asks, "I am curious about that name – Emma."

"That is my name."

He looks at her and stops chewing the berries, then he says, puzzled, "What a strange name. What kind of bird or animal is called ... Emma?"

"I don't think it is a bird or an animal. It's just a ... name."

"How did you get here?" Zehun asks.

"I don't know. I have just found myself ... here."

"Here," he says quizzically "here ... picking berries?"

She looks down, saying nothing.

He looks at the arrows in her quiver. "I see you have new arrows. They are not Hun arrows."

Emma pulls one from her quiver and studies it. "I had them made by an old man in our tribe. Now I can make them myself," she says proudly, marveling how easy it is for her to speak here. *She feels joy, putting flex and feeling into her words.*

"Well now, that's impressive. So you've been practicing?"

"Yes, a lot."

"Who is training you?"

"I listen to everybody."

Zehun nods. "Okay," he says, looking around, eyes narrowing now on the far side of the pond. "See those three ducks? Kill one of them."

Emma follows Zehun's point of view, locates the ducks, and shrugs. She takes the arrow she has in her hand and places it in the string of her bow. She does this while she is standing. Now she steadies herself, and gently pulls back. Then she elevates the angle of the arrow and pulls until the string kisses her lips. Then she lets the arrow go. It lands with a thud *into the center duck. There is instant panic as the other ducks flee.*

"Nice work. You shoot like a Hun."

"I've been working on it," says Emma. "I want to be very good."

Zehun nods approvingly, then observes, "I see you pull left-handed."

Emma looks curiously at her left hand, as if seeing it there for the first time. She squints out over the water. Several ducks have returned and landed. Emma changes the bow to her right side, swiftly reloads an arrow, positions the bow diagonally across her chest, and with her right hand pulls back with amazing speed. A duck erupts in death.

Zehun takes a deep breath, eyes wide with astonishment.

"My last teacher informed me I have two arms," says Emma, "and that they were equal."

Zehun laughs. "You have learned well. We'll get over there before we leave and take those ducks for dinner."

Emma lowers the bow, pleased with her aim.

Suddenly Zehun stands. "Forget the duck. We have to get out of here!"

He extends his hand, and she hesitates, but then takes it. He pulls Emma to her feet. Zehun looks over her shoulder and frowns. "Somebody's coming. Many are coming. We have to go! Forget the berries; get your bow and sword!"

Emma follows Zehun's sight pattern. "I see nothing; I hear nothing."

He gives her a strange look. "Believe me, the Romans are closer than I thought. Let's go now!"

He grabs her and drags her; she is running now beside him, as fast as she can. He takes her through a stand of tall trees, down a bank, along the river, and into an area thick with bushes. He has two horses there. He throws her on one, climbs on the other, and commands, "Follow me!"

In an instant, they are slicing through the forest, branches lashing Emma's face.

"Where are we going?" Emma asks.

"To a safe place. I will take care of you!"

They cross the river at a point where it is shallow and wide. They gallop through the water, and Emma feels it splash up her thighs. It is very cold. Up on the opposite bank now, they gallop up a gentle ridge, which suddenly becomes very steep.

"Grab the horse's mane," commands Zehun over his shoulder.

Soon the land flattens, and they turn and look to the south. Great plumes of smoke are rising at villages strung out along the river. Emma gasps in horror.

"They are scorching the earth," says Zehun, pulling his horse to a halt. "The Romans will leave nothing, except a legion of soldiers to lay claim to the land."

A short time later, Emma says, "Look, they are already where we were."

"But they'll be busy a while. They have much to do, killing, burning. Worse, they'll probably get those ducks!"

As they are watching, Emma asks, "How ... how did you know they were coming?"

Zehun looks at her with a kind of blank stare. "You mean, you don't know?"

"No."

"You people sure are backward down here. My horses told me. They knew the Romans were coming long before we could see or hear them. Their horses sent messages to our horses."

"But ... but your horses couldn't see you. They were in the tall stand of trees."

"Oh, my girl, you do not know the Huns. The horses send us visions *of what they see. A thousand Roman horses were sending visions. Easy for my horses to pick up and send to me. Did they teach you nothing growing up in your village?"*

Emma is speechless. She knows how to do this, but is shocked to be with somebody who also does it so casually and naturally.

Zehun looks surprised. "For us, this is as easy as breathing. We learn to receive the images from horses when we are children. All you have to do is open your mind and listen. It is like opening the flap of a tent, and the breeze comes in!"

"This is very surprising," ventures Emma, at the same time thinking how familiar it all is.

"It is very natural," says Zehun as he swings his horse around, heading farther up the mountain. "I will teach you. Now, we have to get out of here. The Romans will soon send scouts."

"Where are we going?"

"To my homeland. I must go back to my tribe. Attila is dead."

"Dead?"

"Yes," says Zehun over his shoulder. "He's dead. His mighty army is now divided. Factions fighting each other. The lieutenants all scrambling for power. I want no part of that."

"How far is your homeland?"

"Fifty days."

"Fifty days!"

"Are you also hard of hearing? By the time you get there, you will know how to receive and transmit images from the horse the way the Huns do."

"You know, deep down, I think I know how to do that. It's just that ... I never met anybody else who could do it."

Zehun rolls his eyes. "From what I can see, you need to get a lot better at it."

They ride, and then Emma asks, "Why did you come back for me?"

Zehun reins to a stop now and asks, "Isn't that obvious?"

"No."

Zehun sighs, exasperated, then says, "I am finished with fighting. I am going back home to farm, raise goats, make children."

"How are you going to do all that?"

"Which part?"

"Well, making the children. That part."

Zehun rolls his eyes and cocks his head. "That's where you come in. You're going to be the mother of my children – and that is why I saved you!"

Emma opens her mouth to say something, but no words come. There is a cold feeling in her stomach. But she is not afraid, just shocked.

Finally, she is able to speak. "Does that mean I will be your ... wife?"

Zehun shrugs. "If you'd like that, it's fine with me. Being married is not important, at least not to me. I just need you to make babies." He eyes her up and down, then says conclusively, "You look like very fine breeding stock!"

"Wow, how romantic!"

Zehun frowns. "What is this ... romantic?"

"Teach me how the Huns talk with horses, and I'll teach you romance."

Zehun thinks about this for a fleeting second, then says, "You are very, very strange. Like, you are not of this earth!"

* * *

Emma is startled. Somebody is knocking on a door – her door. She is not on a horse galloping through a forest. She is in her bed, at home.

"Emma, your light's still on. It's midnight."

Emma is fully awake now. She looks around the room. Yes, she decides, her light *is* still on.

"Okay, Mother. Fell asleep."

"Okay, my dear, we're going to have a good weekend! I'm taking you someplace very special. Sleep now."

"Mother, first, there is something ..."

Emma climbs out of bed, opens the door, looks her mother in the eye. "Am I see Tower again? Going to ride like before? Love Tower, my horse."

Millie takes a deep breath, then says, "I don't know."

"Why ....? You know everything."

Millie steps forward to give Emma a hug, but Emma steps back. For a long time, mother and daughter say nothing. Deep inside Millie is happy; the old Emma is returning.

Millie levels her gaze at Emma, then she says, "Look, I am sorry about the medication. I should not have told you it was vitamins. I lied. I just didn't want to give you cause to worry."

"It's okay, Mother."

"Love you, Emma."

"Yes…."

"You don't have to take the medication anymore."

"I … I want be … me."

Emma stands silent a moment, then she says suddenly, "I already stopped taking it."

Millie nods. She stifles an urge to step forward and hug Emma, then says: "I see that."

Finally Emma closes the door and returns to her bed, where she lies awake for what seems like forever.

CHAPTER TWENTY-THREE

Sunday, June 27. Allan, Millie, and Emma pull into the gravel parking lot of the Sherman Oaks Rescue Mission for Horses. It is a facility funded by private donations, to link prospective owners with likely horses abused or abandoned. There are also mustangs culled from federal BLM holdings.

Emma's mood elevates immediately she walks through the stalls and out into the holding pens. She is petting horses, so excited to be among so many.

Millie notices that she seems to be communicating once again, but then, she is not sure.

"See what I mean?" says Millie. "She is *so* happy. This is the Emma we love. She is becoming her old self."

"You're right," says Allan, "it's like she's in a candy store, with all these horses."

While Emma is moving among the horses, Allan and Millie converse with the staff. The director says they rotate about a hundred horses in various places, and they do the best they can. They keep horses as long as it takes to find an owner – except if the horses are dangerous. They must be careful about liability, after all! A young assistant, a girl in her early teens, takes Allan and Millie aside, looks furtively around, and whispers, "Then we call the auction people, if the horses are dangerous. And I suspect they sell them for dog food! I hear they eat horsemeat in France. Disgusting!"

Allan and Millie walk through the stalls and out into the pastures. They realize it has been some time since they have seen Emma. They call her. No answer. Millie feels panic rising. She asks a Mexican worker if he has seen a blonde teenage girl. Millie speaks some Spanish, but the worker says, "Yes, girl is in end paddock, where there is loading ramp." He points.

Allan and Millie hurry to the ramp, and they find Emma, who is in a pen with several horses. A stock trailer is backed up to the loading dock. Two men are opening a gate so horses can enter the stock trailer.

"Oh, my God," says Millie, "there's Emma … and there's Tower!"

Emma is reaching up, trying to hug Tower's neck, trying to pull him away from the other horses, away from the stock trailer ramp. Tower is reaching down, giving that deep murmuring sound. The two men are coming forward. One has an electric cattle prod, the other a long dressage whip. They tell Emma she should not be here. They have to load the horses into the trailer.

Now both Millie and Allan are there with Emma and Tower. There is a moment of standoff. The two men are puzzled at this interruption. They have a job to do, load horses to go to the killers.

Emma is still hanging onto Tower's neck, as if glued there, and Tower is murmuring, those low sounds horses give when they are very, very happy.

Emma turns, and what Millie sees causes her to gasp and cup her mouth. *Emma is crying real tears!* Allan sees this, too, and is visibly stunned. Millie rushes forward and hugs Emma. And now she is crying. Allan cannot help himself; he feels he is being choked, and then he too feels his throat closing and tears running down his face. Emma is crying – she has never cried!

"This is the craziest thing I have ever seen," says the man with the cattle prod. "We come to get a killer horse, and we got these people crying like babies."

"Yeah," says the man with the crop, "horse people, they're all weird."

"This horse is not going anywhere," says Allan, his tone even and flat.

"You got that wrong," says the man with the cattle prod. "I just paid six hundred dollars for that there killer, got the paper to prove it."

Allan pulls the Rolex watch off his wrist. "This watch is worth nine thousand dollars. Deliver this horse to my ranch, twenty miles from here, and the watch is yours. Deal?"

The men look at each other, a 50/50 split obvious.

"Well, I guess we could always tell the boss the horse jumped out of the trailer on the freeway! Son of a bitch is crazy enough!"

"Right then," says Allan, "follow me!"

Emma helps load Tower in the trailer, placing him in last, so he will be first out. And then she climbs in after him.

"Hey," says the man with the cattle prod. "You can't ride in there."

"Against the law," says the man with the dressage whip.

"Not my law," says Allan. "She rides in there, and you follow me."

* * *

Riding back home, Tower and Emma exchange pictures. He has had many adventures. Now Emma realizes she is seeing the images sharply. Back home, Emma puts Tower away and goes to bed. She has many emotions. She is completely confused and exhausted, but feeling a rush she has never felt before. She will start working with Tower tomorrow, first over jumps, then taking him up into the mountains, so he can reconnect with the hills. She is so happy knowing he is back in his stable, just five minutes' walk from her door. She thinks of him and invites him to send a picture. There is nothing. She smiles. She knows he is eating. She lies awake for a very long time, and slowly sleep seduces her. In her vision, she sees Jules, and they are by the waterfall, and their embrace moves forward from where they had left off in real time by the waterfall …

CHAPTER TWENTY-FOUR

Saturday, July 3. Jules and Emma are riding toward the waterfall. This time she is on Tower, and Jules is on the mule Rocket. They climb down from saddles and secure the horses. They have sandwiches and drinks. Jules spreads a square tablecloth.

"There," he says proudly. "A real picnic." He reaches off to the side and pulls a couple of purple sage flowers and stands them up against the sandwiches.

"There," he says, "flowers too!"

Emma comes forward and finds herself embracing him. His chest feels so massive and warm against her. Her heart is beating so fast she is sure he must feel it. Suddenly, she realizes how close she is to him, and she backs away, breaking the moment.

Jules recognizes this and says, "You must be happy to have Tower back."

"Very happy. Tower and me, going to work now."

Jules laughs. "Now, there is the Emma I know!"

"Okay," says Emma, "feed me, read to me."

Jules spreads out the food. They eat, talk about horses, and bask in each other's presence.

"I looked up that medicine," says Jules. "It stops the release of natural opiates in the brain and ..."

Emma puts her hand on his and looks at him. "Doesn't matter. Not taking it anymore. Not for three weeks. Visions coming again. Pictures happening with Tower. I feel ... wonderful."

"Wow, that's good. We've got the old Emma back. You sound ...normal!"

He goes to his saddlebags, takes out a book, and reads.

Emma squeezes his hand. Interesting, she thinks, how for so long she hated being touched or touching. At least, in real time. It is always different with Zehun. His world is another world, where she can do things that do not have the same restraints as in real time, this time, this world. She wonders how she could be so different in that world from this world, the world with Jules.

After a while, Emma says, "Explain why Attila so ... cruel."

"He was cruel. But so were the Romans. When they invaded, they took over the country, dominated the people, and forced them to be Romans. Or they killed them. Attila liberated countries the Romans had conquered, and then he moved on. Being brutal was normal for the time ..."

"Do ... you think Attila good man?"

"He was good at what he did. He was the best. When he died, the Huns began their great decline. There was no leader to take over."

"What about … Zehun?" Emma asks.

Jules watches the waterfall. He picks up a pebble and throws it into a backwash. "Well, yes, I've researched a lieutenant named Zehun, and as far as I can learn, he was part of the problem, not the solution. Or at least, it was somebody like Zehun. But there were many Zehuns. It was a common name. Attila had many close lieutenants. No Hun who admired Attila would have liked the Zehun you have described to me. Somebody who killed only armed fighters. Did not rape and plunder. Attila would not have been impressed. Zehun did not induce fear in people. So he was unable to hold the Huns together when Attila died. If this is the Zehun you are talking about."

Jules turns to Emma now, holds her with both hands, and looks deep into her eyes, and she feels her heart stop. He says, "You have a gift, the same gift Attila had. This gift was common among the Huns. They could send pictures to horses, and horses would send images back to them. There are legends where these transmissions went over hundreds of miles. Man and horse did not have to see each other. They just had to 'zero' in on each other, a telepathy. You have the ability to do the same. You send pictures to horses, and they see the same picture. And the reverse is true. I have a little of that, but you … you are much better than I am. I have to concentrate really, really hard, and then it works only sometimes, but you … you do it naturally."

Emma feels herself starting to tremble, and Jules wraps his arms around her.

"I'm scared," she says. "Everybody wanted me to be normal … and now I don't want to be what they call … normal. I was tricked with drugs. Normal was bad! I do not want to be normal, not ever! No drugs. Now I feel I *am* normal!"

"You are gifted," says Jules. "You are beautiful and ... and ..."

Their eyes lock. She feels the softness of his face against her cheek. So incredibly soft. His hot breath in her ear transports her to another place. The heat travels through her brain down her neck, down through her stomach ... and she feels a warmth she has never felt before. Except with Zehun, in the other world. Suddenly, she pulls herself away and holds Jules at arm's length.

"Now," she says after a while, "now I'm scared ..."

Emma looks at Tower. She sees an image of a feed bucket. The image is so clear she can see the edges of the individual grains. She laughs. Jules looks puzzled.

"I see it all now clear as sky. I am thanking Tower for being home now." And to herself she says, "Thanks, Tower, for the interruption. I needed that!"

She stands and tells Jules, "Home now."

Later that night, in her bedroom now, Emma showers, dresses for bed, and flops down on top of the covers. She is tired. She thinks of Jules and wonders about him – how incredible he is, how he gives her strength, how she loves him so dearly. She is bothered by the fact that he looks exactly like Zehun, only in another time. They are, she decides, the same man, only separated by 1,500 years. How could that be? And then, of course, she wonders about Zehun. How is he? Where is he? She remembers the last time they were together, Attila had died, his armies in disarray. She and Zehun were headed for the steppes of Russia, where he was going to farm and she was going to make his babies. She closes her eyes, worried now that it seems necessary that she go back there *urgently.* Something is tugging at her. This time, it happened very quickly, and she was back instantly in that place long ago and far away.

The entrance was startling, and immediate. She is crouched in a cluster of small trees, listening to screams. Somebody is in a lot of pain! She checks her physical presence. She is dressed in deerskin, as usual, and carrying her bow, and the quiver of arrows that Zehun had noted were not Hun arrows. She had told him, quite proudly, that she had made them herself, with help from an older tribesman who knew about pounding copper and dipping the tips of "war arrows" in poison.

Emma looks now in the direction of the screams, and she moves with stealth through the scrub. What she sees makes her freeze. Zehun is tied to a tree, surrounded by Roman soldiers. One of the soldiers holds a bloody knife. Zehun is bleeding from a cut across his chest. He is grimacing in pain. His gold amulet is dripping blood.

"Ah," says one soldier, "now I recognize this man. He is a lieutenant of Attila. What a prize!"

"So," says the man with the bloody knife, "let's kill him! He has killed many Romans, now we'll kill him, only it will take a while ..."

The first Roman soldier shakes his head. "Better idea. The Huns have been extracting mule trains of gold from our beloved emperor. We should take this lieutenant back to Rome, and we will be heroes. We will bring him back alive, and show our emperor that we are smarter than the Huns. I am sure they will make a great event, and feed this Hun to the lions at the Coliseum! We'll see how good he fights then! His bare hands against the teeth of hungry lions. We will get great tribute."

Emma cannot hear this exchange, but she feels something is about to happen. She has an advantage. She has not been discovered. She counts the number of soldiers. Seven. A scouting party, she assumes, that just happened to come upon Zehun when, somehow, she and Zehun became separated on their trek to the Russian steppes. She remembers her horse slid off a path, and she tried to make a wide circle back to the main trail. Now, she is looking through the bushes. She checks her quiver. Seven arrows. She sets an arrow against the string and pulls back at full force so the string kisses her lips as the soldier with the knife is moving toward Zehun. The arrow places exactly where she wanted: in the back of the neck, just below the skull. The soldier drops instantly. Now the others turn, in various degrees of reaction, looking this way and that. Emma fires a second arrow, just a moment after the first. This arrow takes a Roman in the mouth, exactly where she aimed. She fires a third, and it hits a chest. Another arrow drops low, hitting a Roman thigh. Now the other soldiers are running for cover, not knowing from where the arrows are coming. Emma delivers more deadly shots. She is out of arrows, but all the Romans have been hit. Suddenly, a silence settles in.

She moves instantly to Zehun. His face is bloody. He tries to speak, but words do not form. Emma cuts the cords binding him. She looks at him and cradles his face in her hands. "It's going to be okay," she says. "As you are always telling me, let's get out of here!"

Suddenly Zehun's eyes widen. "Look out," he yells, "another Roman coming!"

Emma turns. A Roman is limping toward her, screaming rage, an arrow sticking from his thigh. He has sword in hand. Emma pulls her own sword and stands on guard as the Roman lunges. He is no contest, as he falls clumsily on the leg pierced by the arrow. With every ounce of her strength, Emma swings her sword across his throat, and his head flops back, held in place now only by skin behind the neck. Blood spurts high in the air as he falls to the ground.

Zehun is stunned. "I take back what I said about you and that sword!"

"It was easy. He wasn't moving all that well, with an arrow in his leg."

"You ... saved my life."

"You looked like you were badly in need of saving."

Zehun considers the other Romans, dead or dying. "You got each of them with one arrow."

Emma laughs while she wipes the blood off her sword and returns it to her sheath, then ventures, "Well, Romans are a whole lot bigger than ducks! Like I told you, I've been working on my rapid fire!" She smiles now, enjoying once more how easily words come to her here in this place with Zehun.

"Thank ... you," says Zehun.

"I had to do it," says Emma. "You couldn't father my children if you were dead!"

Zehun drops his head forward and takes hold of the gold amulet hanging on a leather thong around his neck. For a long time he is quiet, as he feels the amulet between his fingers, caressing it lovingly. It is an image of a golden deer, sacred to the Huns. The metal is bright and smooth, worn from years of rubbing on Zehun's massive chest. Slowly he removes the amulet and looks at it in his hand and he is strangely silent. Then he takes a deep breath, as if regaining himself, and he hands the amulet to Emma.

"This," he says, "was given to me when I drew my first blood as a warrior. Now I give it to you, as you have drawn your first blood as a warrior."

Emma is shocked, but she feels him place the amulet around her neck.

"There now," says Zehun suddenly and very serious. "Time to go. I won't father any of your children if we don't get out of here now. That was a scouting party, and another party is out there looking for them. Let's go – we'll find horses. Lots of them running around after this battle!"

CHAPTER TWENTY-FIVE

Saturday, July 10. A jumping show at Trancas Riders and Ropers. Emma is with Tower. Jules is up in the bleachers with his mother, Barbara. Suzanne is also here with Rocket. Tower and Rocket have been trucked to the grounds by Millie and Allan, who are up in the bleachers with Jules and Barbara.

"Emma is real excited to be in competition again," says Allan. "I'll be interested to see how Tower and she go."

"She has been telling me how much she wants to get into competition with Tower, now that she is seeing the pictures again," says Millie.

Allan laughs. "I guess I'm all used to this talking with horses stuff!"

Sixteen riders are in the class. Emma is tenth up. The jumps are set at three feet six inches. Tower easily clears them.

"He's putting about a foot on top of those jumps," Allan observes.

The next go-round, the last jump is set at four feet. Again, no problems for Tower.

"Look how confidently Emma is riding," notes Millie.

"Just like the old days," Allan says.

Emma easily wins the class, with no faults.

There is a round of applause, and Emma does a victory lap, tipping her helmet.

"Well, there it is, ladies and gentlemen, it's Emma Armbrust in the blue. Now give her a hand. It sure is good to have Tower and Emma back! What a team!"

There are hugs all around when Emma exits the arena and dismounts. "That was easy," says Emma. She pets Tower's neck and he makes his happy sounds. "This is what I want to do," says Emma. "I want to compete. Tower loves it!"

CHAPTER TWENTY-SIX

July, the third week. The Armbrusts are stalling the bank – again. They have been given one last extension on the property. Allan has long ago sold his racing prospects. Blazing Light, the last to go, didn't even get a chance to prove if he could run. A great depression has settled over the horse ranch. Specifically, this black cloud has gathered over the kitchen table, where Millie and Allan are sitting over early morning coffee.

"I can't believe we went through $15,000 in just a couple of months," Millie says, dejectedly.

Allan takes a deep breath. "Well, we were behind $5,000 on bills, and $9,000 on the mortgage. Selling Tower just got us caught up, almost."

"Something has to happen," says Millie.

"We'll get through it," says Allan. "We're strong. We're a team."

Suddenly, Allan cocks his head to one side. "Emma must be down in the stable with Tower."

They pick up their coffee, leave the kitchen, and walk out on the lanai overlooking the corral. They are surprised to see Emma approaching, and then clearing, a big fence. As Emma circles around for another jump, Allan is shaking his head in disbelief, then he says, "Look at that horse jump."

"What I'm looking at is the smile on Emma's face," says Millie.

Emma looks up, sees her parents, and waves.

Manuel is there adjusting the poles. Emma indicates she wants an oxer spread – poles spread out twice as long as well as placed high, like a pyramid. While Manuel is doing this, Emma is lying up on Tower's neck, gently stroking him. He is licking his lips and making contented murmuring sounds.

Up on the balcony, Millie says, "I was shocked you gave up your good-luck Rolex." She puts her arm around him. "That is something I thought you would never part with."

Allan nods, as if he had surprised himself. "Well, I won the watch on a horse race the week we met, remember?"

Millie smiles. She remembers all right. It was one of those crazy things men do, two "boys" boasting about their horses at the training track one day down in Texas, and Allan said, "I bet my horse is faster than your horse." The other owner, very successful at that time, took a Rolex off his wrist and said, "If your horse can beat my horse in one lap around the track, this watch is yours. If he can't, your horse is mine. Nothing wrong with that horse that a good trainer couldn't fix!"

Allan ignored the insult. "It's a deal," he said.

Allan's horse won by a length. And so he walked away with a $9,000 Rolex on his wrist.

On the balcony now, overlooking the jumping arena, Allan sips coffee and says, "Well, it *did* turn out to be my lucky Rolex after all! Lucky I had it at the horse shelter. The watch saved Tower."

The oxer is set now, and Emma is trotting Tower around the arena rail.

"Doesn't she have just the most perfect seat," Millie says.

Allan nods. "Yeah, but that's an awfully big jump. Six feet, I'd say. With a twelve-feet spread."

Millie squeezes his arm. "She can do it."

Emma is still circling on the rail. The sun has crested the mountain behind them now, and the air is filled with birdsong.

Allan looks up above the arena, his eyes traveling along the mountains rising up in the distance, their feet in the tide six miles away. "Will you be sorry to lose this place?" he asks quietly.

Millie says, "This means the world to me, but more than anything what makes me happy is having the old Emma back. Look how happy she is. Look how happy Tower is. They are so ... incredible together!"

Allan nods. "You're right there. I am sorry ... I pushed so hard for the medication. I think some of what she has been through is my fault. She was fine all along. Just different."

"It's nobody's fault. You did your best. And if you *did* do anything wrong, you've more than made up for it, believe me."

Allan nods, looking at Emma circling below. She stops to adjust the harness on her crash hat and moves in the saddle, seeking that perfect spot. She is wearing her bright red Tipperary eventing vest, lined with Kevlar blocks. She trots now to the far end of the arena and faces Tower toward the jump.

"My God," says Allan, "I hope she can do this."

Emma moves forward, first at the walk, then the trot, and both she and Tower are a picture of concentration. Emma wears no spurs and carries no crop. She has the reins "breeched" over Tower's neck, her elbows in, heels down, back straight, her body forward just enough to put her head over Tower's front legs, the point of perfect balance. Tower has picked up a canter, an easy, effortless lope. His stride is measured, and five strides out from the jump, he suddenly increases speed. At a point three human strides from the jump, he takes off in a mighty, graceful leap. Emma's hands are forward up on the mane, the reins are loose as flowing ribbons, and her head is up, eyes looking straight ahead, her back parallel to Tower's neck. She does not look down. Tower, it seems, is airborne forever. He clears the jump by four inches, lands, straightens, and slows down, giving a little buck, as if out of sheer joy. Emma drops the reins, throws her arms in the air, tosses her head back, and laughs.

Up on the balcony, Allan drops his coffee mug. It clatters and breaks on the deck. Millie throws her arms around him. They hug, speechless.

Allan says, "I found out why Earl wanted that horse. He was going to enter him in the LA Equestrian Grand Prix in September."

Millie stands back, looks at him, and frowns. "You're kidding. The Grand Prix!"

"No, I'm not kidding. But now, doesn't that give *me* just a smart idea? We'll do it! Purse is $50,000, plus all the other stuff they throw in! And if we can win, it's onto Kentucky and Rolex for $250,000! And then the Masters at Spruce Meadows in Canada, for another million dollars."

"So who was going to ride him, for Earl, that is?"

"Nobody at *their* place," says Allan. "There's nobody anywhere can ride that horse over big fences. Nobody except the girl we're looking at."

And they both look down at Emma, who is taking Tower out of the arena now, to the hitching rail, to be washed and groomed.

"So, you're really gonna do this … really, Allan?"

"Bet your last dollar that's what we're gonna do! It's three weeks before the qualifying event. Doesn't cost much to qualify – just turn up. We still have just enough time to register. He laughs and adds, "There's gotta be something else I can hock!"

Millie laughs, gives him a hug, and says, "Now there's the man I married!"

"Am I better than the actor?"

Millie slaps him playfully. "What actor?"

CHAPTER TWENTY-SEVEN

Sunday, August 15. Emma is sitting at the kitchen table, when she hears about the accident. Millie puts her hand on Emma's arm and says, "Something terrible has happened. Suzanne is in the hospital. She was in a car crash with her mother."

Emma hears the words, but at first can't comprehend.

"It is very bad. Barbara is okay, but Suzanne is …"

"She all right?"

"We don't know."

"Want to see her," Emma says, standing abruptly.

"We can't today. She is in intensive care, UCLA."

"I want see Jules."

"He's not home. He didn't come home last night."

Emma looks at her mother, blinks, then hears herself ask, "Where *is* he?"

"We don't know."

"Take me to his place."

"There's nobody home. They're all at the hospital. They're all with Suzanne … except for Jules …"

Emma spends the rest of the day with Tower. She doesn't ride. She pats him and talks with him, and he looks at her with his deep brown eyes. "Oh," she says, "if only you knew ... Pictures don't work here ..."

* * *

Wednesday, August 18. Barbara reports Jules as a missing person. Police departments from Malibu to Ohio are alerted. No sightings are reported.

* * *

Thursday, August 19. Allan and Millie take Emma to see Suzanne at UCLA. She has regained consciousness, and the doctors have assured Barbara she will recover, but the mending will not be easy. They drove together with Barbara and her husband, Rob.

Emma is shocked when she sees Suzanne. Her head is heavily bandaged. Tubes snake everywhere out of her body. Machines blink.

A nurse checks equipment. "They say it's a miracle," she says. "One strong girl."

Emma holds Suzanne's hand and squeezes. Suzanne squeezes back and smiles awkwardly through her bandages. "I feel like one of those mummies," she says, and then adds, "How is Tower?"

"Normal," says Emma.

Suzanne looks around the room, blinks, and asks, "Where's … Jules?"

The adults look at each other across an uneasy silence.

"We don't know," says Rob, a heavyset man. Rob sells medical supplies and, despite a downturn in the economy, is doing well. He travels constantly, but has called off all work since the accident, which was caused, police said, by a drunk driver.

A bleeping monitor breaks the silence.

"I think we should let Suzanne get some rest now," says the nurse.

* * *

After the hospital visit, Emma goes to her room.

Millie and Allan pour iced tea and sit on the landing overlooking the stables.

"Strange," says Allan, "that the boy would just run off like that."

"Understandable," says Millie. "He just got his world back together, and then it crumbles around him again. I'm sure he'll be back."

"Emma's taking it pretty hard."

"They've been spending a lot of time together."

"So I've noticed," says Allan.

"She'll get out of this funk," says Millie. "Tower is the key. She's back to her old self. You know, I think it's strange that medical science can offer little or no remedy for autism. They seem not to know what it is, much less have a cure. But I swear Tower is changing her in many ways, actually healing her. Sometimes I have to remind myself now that she is autistic. It is like they are partners, Tower and her. He helps her so … so much. She is happy."

"I agree. She does better with the horse than she ever did with the drugs. That's for sure!" Allan admits.

"Good thing," Millie offers.

"A really good thing," says Allan.

CHAPTER TWENTY-EIGHT

Saturday, August 28, early afternoon. Emma is on Tower, galloping up the Santa Monica Mountain Range to the waterfall. She is beside herself with excitement. Jules texted her last night, asking to meet at the falls, pleading with her to tell nobody of his whereabouts.

Emma rounds the last bend now, and there is the waterfall – and Jules. He is dressed in his running shorts. There is no horse. *Odd,* she thinks. *He looks tired.*

Emma climbs down off Tower, and Jules comes forward hesitantly, but actually wanting to rush. There is a moment where they stand off, as if sizing up each other, then Jules says, "Emma, I have missed you."

Emma stiffens. "*Missed* me! Where you been? Everybody searching!"

Jules lowers his eyes. "I am sorry. I ran away."

"Where … you run?"

"An old abandoned cabin, up high above the falls."

"Why … where?"

"I have always wanted to take you there. I have known about it since I was a kid. I have books hidden there. It is where I always ran away before."

Emma stiffens again. She is still holding Tower's reins.

"Why … you run?"

Jules takes a deep breath and finally lifts his eyes. "The accident with Suzanne – I caused it. I was yelling at Mom on the cell phone because of some stupid stuff she said, and then … there was silence."

Emma frowns. "She was hit, drunk driver. Police said."

Jules nods. "Yes, that is what the police said, and that is what the reports said, but that night of the accident, Mom told me to tell nobody about the cell phone call. So I didn't. But it was … my fault. She could have avoided the accident if I had not been yelling at her. She is a very good driver. I distracted her."

Emma takes a deep breath, then says, "You crazy."

"No, no, I just feel bad."

"You run away."

"I'm … sorry," he offers.

"You should be strong … like Zehun." She stiffens, holding herself to her full height, then says, "He never run away."

Jules's head snaps up, as if he has taken an uppercut to the jaw.

"That is ridiculous. I am here now – where the hell is this Zehun?"

Emma looks at him, eyes startled, face expressionless. She climbs down off Tower.

Jules continues, voice rising, "And I'm sick to death of hearing about this Zehun! He is some jerk in your stupid fantasies. I am real. I am here! I'm the one who loves you," he says, raising his voice on each "I."

Emma looks at him, as if seeing him for the very first time. She is searching for words, but finds none. She has never heard Jules yelling.

"And here's something else: I never want to hear you mention Zehun again! I want you to stay in real time. I am the real man; he is some fantasy."

Emma is speechless. And she is suddenly very afraid of Jules as he steps toward her now. She sees he is reaching for her, and he is now holding her shoulders with both his massive hands and shaking her, as if she is a rag doll.

"No … no," she cries. "You hurt me."

"I'm just trying to make you listen!"

Emma knows she must move. She flashes an image to Tower, and she is stepping back now, in that image, and turning to the left, putting Tower between herself and Jules – and in an instant, that is how it happens. Emma gets a foot in the stirrup, Tower turns, and the swing launches her up into the saddle. She gallops off, up the hill.

Safe now, up the hill, she turns, and down there is Jules, running after her, screaming and yelling, arms waving, pleading for her to stop and come back to him. She can barely recognize this man she knows she deeply loves. Why is he doing this? And then, it comes now, that familiar feeling, a place long ago and far away, calling her, "come, come."

And now, looking down a steep hill, she recognizes Zehun. He is at first facing her, as if in recognition that she is there, and then he turns toward Jules, who is rushing now toward him. Zehun is dressed in full Hun military attire, sword at side, bow across chest, arrows quivered at his back.

Emma watches this, puzzled by it all, but knowing she is safe. She is confused because this is all happening here in the hills of Malibu, not at a place long ago and far away. They are there. She is here, on a fast horse, ready for exit. She has a full and clear view. It as if she is right there, but she is actually some distance away.

Jules finally stops, because Zehun, sword drawn, is standing in his path.

Zehun says, "Explain yourself!"

Jules says, "I do not have to explain myself to you. I am trying to save my woman!"

Zehun cocks his head. "Save her? You are threatening her!"

Emma can hear every word, see every expression.

Jules is standing now, catching his breath, his muscles pumped. "I am trying only to make her listen. Why the hell should I explain any of this to you? You're just some jerk in her fantasy. You're getting in the way of my reality."

Zehun half smiles, then says, "For a man with no arms, you talk loud. Emma is my woman. What would she be doing with somebody as worthless as you?"

Jules's eyes narrow, his legs spread in a fighting stance. Veins pop on his neck, his rage is so consuming. "I can kill you with my bare hands. I do not need a sword."

Zehun considers this a moment, then add, as if on afterthought, "You are either very brave, or very stupid." And with that, he tosses his sword, releases a dagger from his belt, sheds his bow and quiver, then steps down off his horse and faces Jules.

Jules smiles, totally relieved that now he has to fight against only bare hands and strength. He remembers his days back at Juvie Hall in Ohio, where absolutely nobody matted him. This will be easy, he concludes. He will inflict massive pain. He is excited, and lusts to break Zehun's bones, one at a time. Now he will fight for Emma! The reality of it hangs in the air like a sky about to open with lightning and rain.

Emma, meanwhile, is watching this from a safe distance. She is in a place where it seems she has no way to get involved. Jules and Zehun are there. She is here. But she sees it all with great clarity. Hears every word. Her heart pounds. Tower is watching this also, but at this time, there is no communication between Tower and Emma. They are merely avid spectators.

The men circle, and Jules in his eagerness makes a rush at Zehun, who is taken by surprise. Jules keeps his momentum going, grabs Zehun by the arm, and literally flips him in the air and over on his back. Zehun lands with a sickly thud. Now suddenly Zehun is energized; he has underestimated his opponent. He circles, regarding Jules with new respect, and then he says quietly, "You know, I love Emma."

Jules shakes his head. "No. Not possible. Because you are not real. I am real. Emma can love only me. And I am going to kill you, if that is what it takes to get you out of her life – out of our life together!"

Zehun flexes, braces himself, and says, "You can't do that, because I am a Hun and you are not. We kill people just because it makes us feel good. You have never killed a single person in your whole life. You've never even killed an animal. You know nothing about killing."

Jules half laughs, and shakes his head. "Well, bad boy, I am Jules Chamberlaine from Malibu, California. I love Emma, and she loves me. She is mine, and you are out of here. There is not enough room on this planet for all three of us. I am going to switch off your lights and punch your clock! Your shift is done, dude!"

They move in on each other, two men of massive strength, writhing, dirt flying – and then, suddenly, Zehun finds his neck in a scissors grip between Jules's powerful thighs. Zehun thrashes this way and that, but it is hopeless. He is "matted."

"So," says Jules, "with just a little twist, I can break your neck."

"So, what's stopping you?"

"Emma has told me you are a man of great compassion. You did not like to kill women and children, which is why Attila never liked you."

"True."

"So I will not snap your neck if you promise to stay out of Emma's life – and my life – and let me be forever with the woman I love."

"Can't promise that. Only Emma can," Zehun gasps.

"Not good enough. I'm sorry but ..."

Zehun coughs, splutters, "You can't kill me, you fool, because I am you!"

"Yeah, right," says Jules, "tell me another fairy tale."

Zehun is breathing heavily, but he gasps, pleading now, "I am you! You are me! We are just in different times."

Jules shakes his head. "This is boring, dude. You are out of here." And he squeezes now with his massively powerful thighs, and then realizes, in horror, that his own breathing is being cut off. The more he squeezes, the less breath he has. The less he squeezes, the more air returns. He is suddenly terrified. He tries again, and it's the same result. He lets go and rolls to the side.

Emma is absolutely mesmerized by what she has seen from up on the hill. The two men she loves, fighting each other.

She has an overpowering urge to gallop down and stop them, but she knows she cannot. What is happening is real, but it is not tangible. The feeling is totally different from what she has always felt going back to that place long ago and far away. She is also conscious of Tower pawing the ground. But there are no pictures. It is like her mind is on information overload.

She watches Jules stagger off back down the hill. Zehun has climbed back on his horse and is about to wheel around – when he stops and looks back at Emma. He studies her for a long time, and then, incredibly, Emma hears his voice, as if he is right there in front of her.

"You must go now, my love. The time has come," Zehun says.

"No, no!" Emma hears herself say. "I want to ride to your home."

"Your home is in the real world," says Zehun. "Make your children with Jules. He loves you. He fought for you. He could have killed me, but he didn't."

Zehun slaps his chest with the hilt of his sword and gives a bloodcurdling Hun war cry, and then he is gone, galloping into the forest.

What Emma hears next is Tower pawing the ground, impatient to be standing there. Emma shakes her head and clears her eyes, as if snapping out of a deep sleep. She looks down the hill to where she had last seen Jules. The trail is empty. She gallops down as fast as Tower can take her. She reins in at the place where she had argued with Jules. She looks frantically around. There is nobody. She waits, feeling her heart pound.

She calls his name. No reply. Then she sees him to her right. He is thrashing through the scrub.

"I'm sorry," he says, gasping. There are scratches on his face, his shirt is ripped. He takes a deep breath and steadies himself. "What I said was not right."

Emma is overwhelmed with relief. "I love you, Jules!"

Jules breaks into a smile and comes forward. "That is music to my ears."

"Believe me," says Emma, "I am hearing the music too!"

Emma slides down off Tower and embraces Jules. "You warrior," she says.

Jules half smiles and is puzzled. "Am I as good as Zehun?"

"Yes. I know this for sure. I saw it!"

Jules looks puzzled, but has no response. He is just happy to be with Emma. "I thought you had galloped home!" Jules says.

They embrace, and over her shoulder, Emma tries to see the trail that was the scene where Jules and Zehun fought. But it is not there. It is gone with Zehun, to that place long ago and far away. She closes her eyes and hugs Jules.

CHAPTER TWENTY-NINE

Saturday, September 11. Allan, Millie, and Emma transport Tower to the Los Angeles Equestrian Center, a sprawling complex off the 134 Freeway, Buena Vista exit. There are thirty-eight horses entered to qualify for the Grand Prix in two weeks. At age eighteen, Emma is the youngest rider. The qualifier is a one-day event to establish that riders and horses have the skills necessary to perform in one of the most dangerous activities in equestrian competition. Entry fee is $50, the purse $1,000.

Allan does not realize the enormity of what he is doing until he is in the registration office. A middle-aged lady with oversized glasses looks up at him. "Are you *sure* this is the event you are entering? There is a Pony Clubs of America show next week …"

"We're here to qualify for the Grand Prix," says Allan. "Emma is older than she looks."

The woman considers the registration form and looks over her glasses at Emma. "Wait one minute," she says finally. She leaves, enters a side office, returns after several minutes, and then announces: "Okay, I guess you can do it. No age restriction in Grand Prix."

The qualifier is open to all riders, all horses. The course is as it will be in the Grand Prix. Fences at five feet six inches, with combinations, oxers, and verticals. There is a draw for order of *go.* Allan is relieved that Emma is number twenty-two, placing her entrance after the lunch break. It will give her time to memorize the course. Emma is excited and seems not to notice the strange looks she is getting from other riders.

"You've got to be kidding," says one lady with a German accent.

"They should be reported to Child Welfare," says another.

And then they see Tower, and there is no hiding the shock on their faces. "A thoroughbred!" gasps a thin man with a clipped British accent. He is holding a set of reins to which is attached a seventeen-hand warmblood, coal-black and massive. "Can't recall when I've seen a thoroughbred in Grand Prix."

"I don't think you'll see it after this qualifier either," quips the lady with the German accent, as she walks past with her seventeen-hand gray Trakehner.

Qualifying rules vary, but mostly each rider has two runs. If no rails fall on the first go, it is up to the judges to decide if a second go is necessary. The object is to make sure that horse and rider are capable.

Stables are busy with grooms, owners, riders. Tension fills the air, barked orders ending on high notes. Allan hears one voice he recognizes. Earl Holloway looks as shocked to see Allan as Allan is to see him.

"What the hell are *you* doing here?" he scowls at Allan.

Allan shrugs. "We've come to qualify for the Grand Prix."

It was as if Holloway doesn't hear this. He looks past Allan and sees Tower, then snaps, "And what the hell is *that* horse doing here?"

"Oh, Tower," says Allan, as if recognizing him there for the first time. He grins. "He's what we're qualifying with."

Holloway grinds out his cigar under a *No Smoking* sign. "And who's the fool riding that killer? He should be dog food right now."

"I'll save a surprise for you," says Allan. He turns and goes back to help Manuel with Tower.

In the arena, the riders walk the course, pacing out from each jump – four human paces being equal to one stride of a loping horse.

"What are they doing?" asks Emma.

"I'm not sure," admits Millie. They are sitting at the front rail while Manuel preps Tower back in the barn under Allan's watchful instruction.

The three judges, sitting in a closed-off area along the rail, look across at Emma. She is wearing her bright red vest and playing with her hard hat. "Come on," says Millie, realizing they have become the center of attention. "Let's do what they're doing." And so they walk the course. "Lock the pattern in your memory," Millie tells Emma.

Emma looks at her, hands on hips. "It's a picture, Mother. A picture! Right?"

"Okay, okay."

The German lady is up first. She salutes the judges, trots in a circle, and starts the course. Her Trakehner moves effortlessly, jumping with a minimum of energy, just enough to cover the poles. Clear round. Judges make notes. The German lady leaves the arena and is met at the south gate by Earl Holloway. "Great go," he tells her.

Next up is a heavyset lady from San Diego. She is riding a Warmblood. She easily clears the first two fences, but knocks a rail on the third. She doesn't seem to notice, and turns now into the combination, three vertical jumps set up so the horse must do two strides between the jumps. The Warmblood clears the first vertical but is badly placed for the second, and he crashes into the poles, gets his legs tangled and goes down nose first. The lady rolls off, arms flying, and lands flat on her back, still clutching the reins. The horse pulls back and runs to the south gate. Two medics rush onto the grounds, but the woman climbs to her feet and stands uncertainly. She is dazed but apparently not hurt.

"She was scared," says Emma. "Horse knew. She looked at the jump; horse stopped to see what she was looking at."

Millie feels a stomach chill. Her mouth goes dry. More than anything now, she wants to take Emma by the hand, leave this arena, and go home. "This is crazy," she tells herself. What was she thinking! She is relieved to see Allan coming toward her. "Well," he announces, "Tower is excited!" He sits and gives Emma a hug. "Lady scared," Emma says again.

The next rider has a clean round and, like the first, is instructed by the judge that she has qualified. No need for a second go.

Another rider, a Spanish man, is eliminated after four refusals. "I want see Tower," says Emma. They head for the stables.

The lunch break is over. Emma is saddled and ready at the south gate. As the rider before her leaves, the judge calls Emma to enter the course. Allan pats her on the leg. "Good luck, girl. You're the best."

Emma looks down at him and says, as if on an afterthought, "I'm not best. Tower is best."

Emma pictures the course in her head. She knows Tower is seeing this picture too. It is image-sharp. She moves in a wide, warming-up circle. Tower feels light and responsive, so relaxed Emma wonders if he is taking this seriously. He does a flying lead change and snorts, the way he does when he is amused by what Emma is thinking. She aims him at the first fence, approaches, and looks to a point two strides out. Tower is looking at that spot also, and that is where he heads. The jump is clean and easy. Emma pictures herself clearing the next jump, and it is as if Tower then moves into the picture, clearing it just as she had imaged. Jumps speed by, images of the course playing over and over in Emma's head. Picture, jump; picture, jump; picture jump. Into the triple now, and Tower is caught half a stride off where he should have been, in the same position now as the horse ridden by the heavy lady. Emma feels this, but sees a picture of Tower jumping massively, and more vertically. And that is exactly what he does – a correction only possible by a superb athlete, and a rider who feels no fear, no panic. Coming into the final oxer now, Emma sees a picture of her and Tower riding out of the south gate, the course finished, not a single rail touched. Somewhere before that picture, Tower clears the final jump. Emma is unaware the judges are standing and clapping, as are spectators sitting around the arena. Emma falls on Tower's neck and hugs him with all her strength. He paws the ground. Feed me, he is saying.

* * *

At home, the night after qualifying, Emma goes to her room, locks the door, and opens the bottom drawer. Jules has given her many books on the history of the horse. She looks at them as if seeing them for the first time. She closes her eyes and hears Jules's voice. He is reading to her, in her mind, about a time long ago and far away, when men on horses crashed into each other, women and children screamed, the heavens split with thunder, blood flowed, and wild beasts howled at the moon; but there, always, somewhere, was Zehun, to save her, as he always did, his massive arms plucking her easily from danger. But this night she does not go back to that place far away and long ago. She is happy with that, however. She wonders why seeing Zehun used to be so important, but now it is not, she tells herself. He was in a time and place far away, and perhaps he was not real at all. Yeah, she tells herself again, Zehun is not real. Jules is real. Forget Zehun.

CHAPTER THIRTY

Sunday, September 12. Earl Holloway's ranch in Thousand Oaks. Lewis Williams, on crutches, is negotiating the door to Earl Holloway's oak-paneled office in the main house. Williams knows this is a serious summons because anybody called to this room is invariably fired, threatened, or otherwise made to feel very uncomfortable. Earl is seated at his large swivel chair, a cigar firmly clamped in the corner of his mouth. "Sit," he snaps at Williams. Earl's chocolate Lab, Diesel, is standing by his desk to the left. Diesel shoots a glance at Holloway and sits immediately.

"We have a problem," snarls Earl.

"Yes, sir," says Williams, as his rear end connects with a chair and his crutches clatter to the floor.

"Tower was jumping the moon at the Equestrian Center yesterday."

Williams is shocked. "We off'd that horse, sir. Sent it for an appointment with the killers. Did it myself, sir!"

Holloway's eyes narrow. "Did you see him loaded in the killer trailer?"

"Well, not exactly."

"You're a fucking incompetent idiot!"

"I don't understand…."

Holloway leans forward, taps the ash off his cigar, and considers it as it lands on the carpet. He glares up at Williams. Diesel glares at him too. "Well, he ain't dead, that son of a bitch. The Grand Prix is coming up, and I do not want to see Tower in the lineup. Emma and Tower have qualified, for chrissake!"

Williams considers this. "Well, we could buy them off … sir. They need the money."

Holloway glares at him. "You're as dumb as a rock. That won't work. I've spent enough money on that horse. Your medical bills alone!"

"Well, I've got some other ideas, sir …"

"Please share them," says Holloway, rocking back in his chair and sending a huge cloud of smoke toward the fresco ceiling. "If you do not have a good idea, then you're on the next flight back to London."

"Okay, sir, this is what I have in mind …"

Holloway cuts him short. "First off, I don't want to know exactly what your plan IS. I just want to know you *have* a plan! I just want you to *do* it."

"Yes … sir."

"Am I perfectly clear?"

"Yes, sir!"

"A clean job, no trails."

"Copy that, sir!"

CHAPTER THIRTY-ONE

Friday, September 24. A soft dawn light spills over the Armbrust farm, high in the Santa Monica Mountains. The night before, Allan had loaded the tack in the forward section of the small two-horse trailer, the only trailer left now on the property. The week before he had sold his stock trailer to fetch the $600 entry fee for the Grand Prix and to overnight a check to the Edison Power Company before they shut off ranch power. Millie has packed their clothes in two suitcases in the back of the '92 Dodge Cummins one-ton, with 400,000 miles on the clock. Manuel is there too, but suddenly, he announces, he will not be going. Allan is puzzled. He shrugs off questions in his mind. He will call on friends for help when he reaches the Equestrian Center. Still, Allan can't help but think it odd that Manuel would excuse himself at such a critical moment. Forget it, he decides. Time is running out. He plans to be at the Equestrian Center later in the morning to get Tower settled in over the rest of Friday, and all Saturday, before the Grand Prix on Sunday.

Allan loads Tower, climbs into the truck, and they all drive off down North Kanan Dume Road, headed to the 101 Freeway. North Kanan Dume just happens to be one of the steepest main roads in California. Coming out of the second tunnel, Allan downshifts into second gear, not trusting the brakes. Suddenly, coming up on the left side, a beat-up old Ford sedan swerves in front. Allan swears and whips the wheel to the right, to avoid a collision, but then he has to whip back violently to the left to avoid running into the side of the hill. He looks in the rearview mirror and is horrified to see that the trailer has, incredibly, sprung loose and is skidding sideways into the hill, where it comes to rest with a sickening thud. Millie is screaming. Emma is making strange choking noises. Allan scrambles from the cab, runs back to the trailer, and climbs up through the side door. "He's down," he yells. "Tower is down!"

The trailer careened to a stop at a forty-five-degree angle, and the top slammed against the vertical rock bank. The towing shaft housing the hitching ball is stuck into the rocks and the soft earth. Allan struggles with the back tailgate, and he now realizes there are other hands helping him. Two strong young surfers are pulling with him. They've parked their Jeep on the uphill curb. Surfboards are lashed to the top.

"Holy shit," says one. "Hey, dude," says the other, "we gotta get that horse out o' there!"

Finally, the tailgate drops, hinges straining against an awkward angle. Allan climbs in. Tower is motionless, save for a twitching in his back leg. His eyes are half closed, and blood is flowing from a cut on the top of his head. "He's out cold," says Allan. "Millie, somebody, call 911."

A fire truck arrives. Sirens blare. The Highway Patrol is there now, directing traffic. With the help of even more motorists, they manage to right the trailer, and it lands now with all wheels on the ground.

"So," asks the Highway Patrol officer, "what happened?" The officer is a very large African American. But before Allan can answer, the officer is studying the hitch. "No safety chains," he observes.

Allan shakes his head. "I put them on," he says. "I ... I always do. But ... but what happened was a car swerved in front of me. To avoid hitting him, I had no place to go but into the bank, and when I cut back, the trailer ... was ... gone."

"Did you get a license plate number?"

"No ... it all happened so fast."

"Description of vehicle?"

"Dark brown, beat-up, like one of those Escorts."

The police officer rolls his eyes. "Only about half a million of those in LA County."

From inside the trailer comes Emma's measured voice. "No license plate. Station wagon. Rusty gray, roof silver. Rust all over. Silver tape on taillight. Long crack in back windshield ..."

The officer frowns, looks into the trailer, and sees Emma cradling the head of the horse in her lap. "Hey," he says, "you seem to know a lot about that car."

Emma just gives him a blank look.

The officer steps down, shaking his head.

"She's autistic," says Allan. "She sees stuff like that in pictures. She sees *everything*!"

The officer frowns, rolls his eyes, and in a public relations tone says, "Quite all right, sir."

The officer looks closer now at the trailer hitch. "The lock pin is out as well," he says.

Allan looks in disbelief. "I ... I don't ... understand."

The officer looks around. Traffic is backed up in both directions. He talks on his lapel radio, then announces, "Here, hitch this trailer up again and get out of here. Attend to the horse when you get the trailer to a safe place."

Allan hitches the trailer, places the latch pin, secures the safety chains, and goes back to look at Tower. Millie and Emma are in there with him. Millie is weeping, but Emma is strangely calm. She has Tower's head still cradled in her lap, and she is rubbing his neck.

"Come on!" snaps the police officer. "Get this outta here now, or I'll be writing you a ticket!"

Millie comes out of the trailer, but Emma refuses to leave. Tower is breathing heavily, massive chest rising and falling. He is still on his side, wedged there. Allan had moved the divider to the other side to make room for Tower to get up. Allan curses now, lifts up and locks the trailer ramp, attaches the safety chains, climbs into the cab, and drives to a shaded pull-off area at the bottom of the hill.

"What happened to the trailer?" Millie asks for the third time.

Allan turns off the engine. "No idea," he says. "All I know is I put the pin in place and I secured the safety chains. I've done it a thousand times, for God's sake!" He lets his head fall on the steering wheel. "What I want to know is what the hell that car was trying to do!"

"It looked … intentional," says Millie.

Allan curses under his breath. "The safety chains were unhooked, the lock pin out. Yeah, I'd say it was intentional! Somebody messed with my trailer."

While Millie is again trying to contact the vet, Allan goes back into the trailer. Emma still has Tower's great head in her lap. She has used her gym jacket to wipe the blood off his forehead. "Wants water," she says. Allan fetches a bucket from the front of the trailer and fills it with water from a thirty-gallon dispenser. Emma dips her jacket in the water and wipes Tower's head. His head jerks up, then falls down again.

"The vet is on the way," says Allan.

"He's … all right, Daddy."

"You think so?"

Emma nods. She puts her head on his cheek and speaks quietly to him. He trumpets softly, that sound he gives when he understands. And Emma says, "It's okay. Tower resting now …"

Dr. James Swank arrives twenty minutes later. He has treated the Armbrust horses for years, and on occasion has looked at Tower – for worms, an abscess in the hoof, and, once, a strained stifle.

"Hello, Emma."

Emma nods.

Dr. Swank places the stethoscope in his ears, listens a minute, and says, "Heart rate is good. Breathing is good. He's going to be okay." He bends and places a probe light over Tower's eye. "Nasty cut, but the eye is okay."

Emma nods. "I know …" And then she stands quickly, but not in a panic. Tower is lifting his great head, and the doctor backs out of the trailer. Now Tower is standing, swaying unsteadily at first, but quickly balancing and planting his feet. His off-side eye is half closed, but the bleeding has stopped.

"What do you think?" Allan asks.

Dr. Swank doesn't answer immediately. He is checking the damaged eye. He runs his hands over Tower's legs, feeling for bumps. He takes another heart reading. And then he says, "Well, no broken bones. Just all shook up. He's taken a pounding, lost a bit of hide here and there, and that eye, that's gonna close. But no permanent damage that I can see."

Dr. Swank goes to his truck, pulls out a syringe, and fills it with a clear liquid. "But," he says, "this'll help his headache." He feels for a vein in Tower's neck, and pumps. "So, where's Tower going this morning?" He removes the needle and dumps it in a waste container in his truck.

Allan says, "We're doing the Grand Prix this weekend at the Equestrian Center."

Dr. Swank shakes his head. "Grand Prix? I don't think so. He'll have only one eye working tomorrow!" He shrugs, pulls out an alloy clipboard, writes up a bill, and hands it to Allan. "Pay when you can," he says. "And good luck!"

And so they continue south on the 101 Freeway, to the 134, to the Buena Vista exit, and into the Los Angeles Equestrian Center. Emma is riding in the back of the trailer with Tower. She refuses to leave him. They are directed to Tower's stall. They unload. Allan is relieved that Tower is walking fine, no limps, but the off-side eye does not look good. It is now almost completely closed. As Tower is being led to his stall, he is cocking his head to the right so the one good eye, on the near side, has a field of vision.

When Tower is settled in his stall, Allan uses a butterfly bandage to close the cut above Tower's eye. Millie is there now with ice in a cloth. Emma is holding the halter and patting Tower's neck. "He's going to be all right," says Emma. For three hours, they treat the eye with the cold press. Tower is eating, and Allan notes, "He's in no pain."

The sun is setting now; the wind is chill, but the parking lot asphalt is still giving off heat from the day. As they sit out by the trailer – Millie, Allan, and Emma – the realization of what they have been through hits. "We're lucky he didn't do a lot more damage," says Allan, pulling a cold beer from the cooler. To lighten the mood of the moment, he proposes a toast. "This is to a great horse … and a great team. Tower can do more with one eye than the rest of them can do with two!"

"Where is Jules?" Emma asks.

"He'll be here," says Allan.

"Are you sure?"

"Sure, I'm sure. Why wouldn't he be? *You're* here!"

"Don't think about Jules now," says Millie. "Think only about winning. You have a big job starting tomorrow. You have to ride Tower in the practice arena, and get him used to all the other horses and the excitement."

"And no jumping," says Allan. "All we don't need is for him to pull something. We need him fresh for Sunday."

Emma looks at her parents, from one to the other, and just shakes her head.

"Wish Jules was here."

"For God's sake," snaps Allan, "he'll get here!"

Millie shoots Allan a disciplinary glare, then puts her arm around Emma.

"Miss him," says Emma. She wonders if Jules is still hiding up in that shack in the mountains. She is full of remorse about the quarrel. Jules wanted only to explain, she decides. Of course, she did not tell her parents about meeting with Jules. She just hoped now he would be over it all, and be here for her.

Millie attempts to tighten her arm around Emma, but Emma moves away.

Millie ignores the rebuff. "Yes, we know you miss Jules. But he'll be here."

"Hey, you have Tower," offers Allan, mustering an upbeat tone.

CHAPTER THIRTY-TWO

Sunday, September 26. The PA system crackles, and the order of *go* for the autumn Grand Prix is announced. Emma is third to last. It is a beautiful southern California day, sunny but not hot, sky clear and blue. Flags flutter, tables are set around the vast arena, parking lots full. Emma is in her white jodhpurs, black boots, red vest. Daylight finds Tower's eye swollen, a little less than it had been during Emma's casual riding around the center yesterday. She had stayed out of the arena with the practice jumps, and tried to keep a low profile with the other riders and the various officials.

Allan studies the eye, then announces, "The ice and the butterfly bandage did great duty."

"Where did you learn that trick," asks Millie, indicating the bandage.

"Oh," says Allan, "learned it a long time ago, back when I was a kid in Battle Creek boxing with the Jimmy Sharman troupe. I got a cut over the eye, and that's how they fixed it."

Emma walks the course with the other riders, counting their adult steps between the jumps, rather than her own. It is obvious to her that the other riders are treating her with respect.

Emma is relieved to see the course is much the same as it had been for the qualifying practice run, except for the addition of a water jump. A three-foot-six jump set up before a ten-foot body of water trapped in blue plastic. She realizes now that Tower has never jumped water, save for small running creeks in the Santa Monica Mountains. For a long while, she stands in front of this jump and studies the water. Tower would have no opportunity to do this jump except for real. She walks around the jump, looking at it from different angles.

Outside the south gate, a practice jump is set up – a single rail at five feet five inches. Already horses are working the jump. Some knock the rail.

Now the announcer's voice fills the air. Next, high notes deliver the national anthem. And the first of twenty-four riders enter the arena.

While Allan watches Tower, Emma and Millie take an arena seat. Emma watches intently as the first horse clears the course, dropping a rail on the very last jump. The challenge to this particular course is the tight angles from two of the jumps, one leading into a giant oxer and another into the triple set at five feet. Even more challenging, the triple is placed near the exit gate. The temptation proves too much for the third horse, and instead of making the sharp left turn into the triple, the warmblood bolts through the gate and is off-course.

"Okay," says Emma, "I've seen enough."

Mother and daughter return to the barn. They do not talk. Emma is aching to ask her mother when Jules is going to appear. But she restrains herself. Her mother has told her to think only of the ride.

Emma and Millie are almost at the barn when Emma gets a text message: Jules is on the way! Emma grabs her mother and gives her a big hug.

"Wow," says Millie. "Such excitement for the ride!"

Allan is sitting on a tack box at Tower's stall. The horse has his nose in a bucket of feed in the far corner, but his head shoots up when Emma approaches. Tower moves across and pushes his head over the half-door, and he makes a low, soft sound. He and Emma exchange images as she rubs the sweet spot on the curl of hair in the center of his forehead. The eye is now almost normal. Alan has removed the elastic bandage and replaced it with a thin line of Super Glue.

"Well, what do you think?" Allan asks.

"Tower okay," replies Emma.

"What about the water jump? He hasn't seen *that*."

Emma looks at her dad, surprised. "Showed it to him."

* * *

Emma is mounted and ready now, at the practice jump, watching the German lady on the gray Trakehner clear the course. The horse had spooked at the water jump, then chipped in and with one mighty leap, cleared the pond.

"That horse," the announcer is saying, "is now the one to beat."

Two more entries before Emma. She is looking now at the practice jump and wondering if she should take it. The jump is a single rail at five feet. There is no jump more difficult for a horse than a single rail, because there is no frame of reference for height. Tower is studying the practice jump as Emma becomes aware of two people walking toward her. One has a clipboard and an air of authority. The other is in a white coat, a stethoscope around his neck.

Emma studies them, and then she hears the official introduce herself. She does not catch the name. She is seeing an image from Tower. He does not want to do the practice jump. The picture he sends Emma is of the first jump on the course.

"This is Dr. King," says the official, her voice terse. "We have come to inspect the eye of this horse. We have a report of injury and possible interference of sight and…."

"He's … he's fine."

"We'll let the doctor decide that. It's about safety, *your* safety, young lady, and the safety of this horse."

The man in the white coat moves forward as Emma hears her name called over the loudspeaker, and she sees the arena gate open. For a moment, she is confused. Why are they trying to stop her while her name is being called? Tower sends the image again of the first jump, which he is clearing easily. He is sidestepping now, agitated at being held back. He is pawing with his hooves and making impatient snorting noises. The official and the doctor quickly move back as Tower swings around and heads for the gate … as Emma hears a familiar voice, "Emma, ride like hell!"

She looks over, and there's Jules, leaning on the rail and waving.

Emma feels her heart leap in her throat.

"Jules, Jules!" she yells.

"Go, go!" Jules yells. "Let Tower *go!*"

Emma turns back to the course and focuses on the first jump as she feels Tower lift up under her. He clears it easily. Emma is locked in concentration as she replays in her mind, like flash cards, the jumps fast approaching. After each jump, she locks her mind onto the next, and Tower is right there. He sends back to her a picture of him clearing the jump an instant before he leaves the ground. Emma feels Tower's might carrying her as if she is weightless. Heading for the oxers now, over which Emma could see the south gate, a temptation that had claimed three horses already in lost time, as their riders were forced to turn their mounts around and reset them for the triple to the left.

Now Tower flashes an image of him clearing the oxers and heading past the gate and onto the triples, actually increasing speed on the tight left turn. He takes the two bounce strides with ease, turns another sharp left to a single five-foot rail, and then around to the right again. All the while, Emma is playing the course through her mind and transmitting this to Tower. Always he is one jump ahead. Never in her life has she felt so in sync with Tower. It is as if they are one. Incredibly, she feels Tower increase speed even more as he takes five fences placed at different spread distances along the north fence. Around to the right now, turning in a tight circle, and Emma is approaching the water jump at full gallop. Suddenly panic catches in her throat as she sees the sun reflecting off the water. The image Tower sends back is one of blinding light. There is no jump, just the light. It is like a torch into Emma's unusual brain. She hates bright lights! Somewhere in the light, the jump is rushing toward her, and she is trying to see through it. She feels Tower catching his stride, as if uncertain, and still the image he is sending is of a shimmering light, a burning light.

No picture of a jump! Now suddenly the jump is there, just two strides ahead, a split second in time at this speed. Emma squints, and in the next instant, she sees the rail, the sun now at a less reflective angle. Tower sees it too, as he is just one stride from the jump. Emma feels every muscle in Tower's massive body explode, as she shoots up high on the jump and is carried over the water by his incredible speed.

But Emma feels herself being unseated by this powerful leap, and she is now on Tower's neck, her fingers clutching desperately at his mane. And then her ears fill with another strange noise. Time seems suspended as she tries to identify this noise, and then realizes it is a mighty, collective *moan* from the crowd. Emma has a death grip on Tower's mane, trying to push herself back in the saddle. She feels herself slipping to the left, but now Tower side-passes to the left, putting his body under her. Then, suddenly, she is slammed back, as Tower makes a mighty leap forward, the jump behind them. Emma is in control again as Tower crosses the finish line, and now the crowd is standing and cheering and the announcer is running over his own words, so incredulous at such a performance. In thirty years, he is saying, he has never seen such a recovery. The crowd is wild – standing, cheering, and clapping.

The announcer's voice booms with enthusiasm, "And there, ladies and gentlemen, you saw a horse actually *save* a rider!"

As Emma is exiting the south gate, she hears the words. "And there you have it. The new leader is Emma Armbrust on Tower. What a horse! What a rider! What a combination!"

As Emma is exiting the south gate, a steward stands in her way and directs her back to the arena. "A lap for the crowd, please," he commands. Emma looks back as she hears a familiar voice. It's Jules, calling her name. For a moment, Emma thinks this might be another vision. But then she sees Jules jumping up and down and pumping the air with his fist. "Yes! Yes!" Jules yells, and Emma sees other people looking at him, and she knows it is *real*.

"Please, madam," the steward yells at her again, "one lap around the arena so the crowd can salute you!"

More wild, out-of-control cheering as Emma takes Tower now at flat gallop around the arena. Tower flashes a picture of his nose in a feed bucket. Emma pats him on the neck, and then they exit. Now Jules is there, slapping her leg. "Awesome," he is saying, "just awesome!"

"Where … where have you been?" Emma asks.

And now Allan and Millie are there. "Great job," he says, "You did it, girl!"

Emma looks down at her father, and he has tears in his eyes. They walk with Tower to the barn, Millie and Allan and Jules. Emma feels like she is floating on air, the cheering of the people fading as the barn closes around her.

Back at the barn, Emma and Jules and Allan and Millie all embrace as one. Tears flow, and Tower snorts that low, happy sound as he buries his nose in a feed bucket.

Allan is distracted by the sight of an official running toward him. "Excuse me," says the official. "It's not over. The Trakehner just came in with the same points as Tower. It's too close to call under the set of rules in this particular Grand Prix."

Allan is puzzled. "What … what does that mean …?" And then, he adds, "The Trakehner. That's Earl Holloway's horse!"

"You're right."

"It means a runoff," says the official. "This is in accordance with the rules assigned to this particular Grand Prix, as sanctioned by the US Federation."

"We gotta go … again?"

"Afraid so. Better get that horse ready. You have five minutes."

Emma is confused at first, but then the reality hits her. She looks at Tower as she runs the course through her mind one more time. Tower snaps his head out of the bucket. He received the pictures. "Sorry!" Emma says. She knows Tower is confused by the pictures she is sending. The course! The water jump!

Tower is not happy. He flashes Emma a picture of the grain bucket.

And for a while they stand there, silent, girl and horse. All others around them are locked out of this exchange of pictures.

Emma looks up over her father's shoulder. She sees the vet and the official entering the barn at the far end, at the south entrance. The purpose in their stride tells her this is not good, and then she hears the vet yell, "Hey, we have to check that eye!"

Emma snaps, "Jules … Daddy … tighten cinch. *Please, now!*"

"Hey, what's the rush? We've got a few minutes!"

"No, now, *now*!"

Jules has already tightened the cinch. He grabs Emma's lower leg and hoists her up, literally throwing her into the saddle.

Emma swings Tower around and bolts for the big door at the other end of the barn, the north entrance. Behind her, an official is yelling, "Hey, you, wait a minute … *wait*! You can't run that horse. We need a vet check on the eye!"

Emma hears her father in heated conversation. *Good*, she thinks, *he is stalling them!*

Emma passes the Trakehner on the way to the arena. He has finished his second run, and there were no rails down, she hears the announcer so inform the crowd.

Allan is running beside Emma as she approaches the arena. "You can win, but you need a faster time and no rails down!"

The announcer's voice says, "Incredible! We have a runoff under the rules of this event. Two tremendous horses here today!"

And then, he says, "But look here, ladies and gentlemen. We have the challenger. It's Emma and Tower … a big thing to ask, but … can they do it again?"

Emma notices the gate attendant snap a radio from his belt and then look up, suddenly concerned. He has received some orders, obviously. She sees him reach for the gate *and he closes it*! For an instant, Emma is confused, bewildered. Why are they locking her out? But then, Tower flashes her a picture. *He is jumping the gate! Oh my God*, she thinks. *This is the Trancas arena all over again!* She settles back in her saddle, feeling his massive power, and he clears the five-foot gate as if he has wings. Now they are on the course!

The crowd is standing. The announcer is unintelligible above the cheering. Emma circles around now, ignoring everybody and instead focusing on the course. The crowd settles down, mesmerized. Emma gives Tower a steady stream of images of him passing over jumps at incredible speed. He flashes back confirming images, but she still has the feeling he is mad at her. She flashes a picture now of his favorite snack – barley and molasses horse cookies. A whole big bucket of them! Tower does a little buck that takes Emma by surprise, and then he is off, approaching the first jump now so fast Emma can feel the wind pulling tears from her eyes. He wants out of here!

And suddenly, she is afraid, very afraid. Tower feels her fear communicating to him through her legs. He sends her an image of clearing the last jump. And she feels a rush of relief.

There now, right in front of her, finally, is the water jump. But there is no sun, no reflection. As if to show off, Tower puts four feet of air over the jump and lands a good ten feet past the far shoreline of the water. Then Emma hears the crowd roaring, and somewhere, that familiar voice: "And there you have it, ladies and gentlemen, a clear winner, by an incredible 2.3 seconds! What a great, great ride on a great, great day! And I must say, in all my years, I have *never* seen such an entrance to Grand Prix!"

Emma heads for the south gate, but the same official who had shut the gate, points her in the direction of a victory lap. He is tight-lipped, and he glares at her. They gallop off around the rail, and this time the tears flowing down Emma's face are tears of joy.

Allan and Millie and Jules are standing, arms raised in triumph. All around them, wild cheering erupts.

Allan and Jules grab Millie and sit her down. Allan says, "Better believe it, $50,000 right there – and it's only the beginning!"

Millie looks at him and blinks. "The beginning? You mean, we'll be doing this again?"

"Yeah, baby! Tower's next stop – Rolex and $250,000! And then Spruce Meadows for another million. We're gonna save the farm, by God!"

They leave the stands and meet Tower and Emma at the exit gate. "You did it, you did it!" Allan explodes.

"No," says Emma. "Tower did it."

And, once again, they walk back toward the barns.

Allan stops suddenly, and as if on an afterthought, reaches out and takes Jules by the arm as Millie leads Emma and Tower back through the barn doors.

"Hey, young fellow, where the hell have *you* been?"

Jules looks down. "I'm sorry, Mr. Armbrust.... I just ... got overwhelmed with everything."

"You caused us all a lot of worry."

"I'm sorry. I … I …"

"Well," he says, "it's just not good enough. You're not a kid anymore; you're supposed to be a man now. You're one of us! So man up! We don't do stupid stuff like that. Get with it!"

Jules lowers his head and feels a great shame. "I'm … sorry."

Allan takes a deep breath, and then in a new voice says, "Okay, okay. You're here now. You showed up. That's what counts."

Now Jules looks up, holds Allan by the arm, and looks him straight in the eye. "Mr. Armbrust, I am in love with your daughter."

Allan jerks back his head, like he has taken a punch. He opens his mouth to say something, but no words come out. Finally, he says, "Well, why the hell don't you tell *her* that!"

Jules turns toward the barn, but Allan steps in his path and says softly, "Just one more thing, then. If you're gonna be involved with my daughter, don't screw up again, hear me?"

"Yes, sir," says Jules and runs toward the barn.

Emma is off Tower now, and Millie is filling a feed bucket.

Jules takes Emma in his arms, aware that Millie is looking back and that Allan is walking toward them.

"I love you, Emma," he says, looking deep into her eyes. "I want to be with you forever and ever!"

Emma hugs him. She feels tears rolling down her hot cheeks.

Jules looks over Emma's shoulder. He is aware Millie and Allan are staring at them. Jules leans forward and whispers in Emma's ear, "Tomorrow, six o'clock. Meet you at the waterfall. I want to propose something really, really special."

Emma looks at Tower, then back at Jules. She moves toward Tower and uses him as a shield from the others. She strokes Tower's neck as Jules is standing there, and then she says, to Tower, "I love you, Jules."

Tower gives a low trumpeting sound, the way happy horses do, and then Emma sees Zehun riding off up a steep hill, in a place long ago and far away, and he is waving good-bye and smiling. He is happy, and Emma knows he is heading back to the steppes to raise crops, milk goats, and keep her memory forever. But he will not be raising her children. And Emma is happy with that.

She is conscious now of Jules looking at her, frowning with concern. "Are you okay?" he asks.

Emma turns, takes him in her arms, and says, "Just drifted off there to a place that is long ago and far away. I saw only you. I love you, Jules."

CHAPTER THIRTY THREE

At home now, in her room, Emma is so happy she feels lighter than air. Tower has been put away, calm and fed. Emma is delirious with joy and wonder. She and Tower made it to the big time! Her heart warms with the thought that she and Jules are back where they were, only now more deeply in love. She smiles at the wonder of her life and decides, just one more time, to go to the secret drawer and study the lithographs and she knows she will find deep contentment to discover no more visions of the Huns, closing forever a chapter in her life, and realizing it was all just a beautiful fantasy. She pulls open the drawer, smiles confidently…and then notices the edge of something bright and very yellow. She frowns. Her heart stops. She pulls back the lithographs and there it is, the gold amulet Zehun had worn around his neck, and given her for taking her first blood.

THE END

Footnote: Earl Holloway filed a complaint demanding Emma be disqualified for her "dangerous and unorthodox entry," but no rules could be found to support a protest about style of entry.

(Quotes for the last pages of the book)

Colin's book is the most unique and innovative insight into human and horse interaction of my acquaintance. It also proposes striking insight regarding autism and may open more avenues to encourage the therapeutic potential of equines and children. It provides remarkable insight regarding evolution of the brain. This is a fascinating landmark and should expand our thinking about the "extrasensory" communication among mammals.
Henry Curry, MD

Bloody marvelous. Most entertaining history lesson I've ever had. You've really done it, Colin. *National Velvet* meets *Love Story* meets the *Horse Whisperer* meets the *Charge of the Light Brigade*. This is terrific. I couldn't have imagined how you could tie Emma's story and the history of the horse together – and you have!
Derryn Hinch, Australia

The writing style reminds me of Hemingway. After reading this book, I may never look at a horse the same way again – because I know the horse will be "reading" me! Great job!
Bonnie Bjehle, Australia

Mr. Dangaard has created a fictional story and characters, and then masterfully interwoven them with factual, historical events and figures. A thoroughly enjoyable read as both an entertaining and educational work.
Emma, the main fictional character, gives us a view into her world of autism, a very complicated, often perplexing condition.

You will walk away with a greater appreciation of the healing power of horses, maybe even the ones in your life.
Jane Lee Beard
Connecticut Horse Council

The theme that Emma's autism might be considered a "gift," rather than a handicap, succeeds. The explanation about how the human brain evolved affecting our interaction with animals and how autism affects human behavior were woven into the fabric and dialogue of the story quite well. Emma's transitions from her present day to historical experiences were smooth.
Stefanie Ward
Anthropologist

Colin Dangaard has the amazing ability to get inside the head of a horse. He communicates with them on a level that is complete. I have seen him work with many horses and they all have one thing in common: they never fear him. It is no surprise that he has written this remarkable work about the depths of communication possibilities between humans and horses. When Colin rides a horse, he becomes part of the animal, and they willing give him their best. He is also a hopeless romantic, so the love story here rings true.
Mara Somma, Calabasas, California

ABOUT THE AUTHOR

I met Colin Dangaard, appropriately, on horseback in 1979. I had heard of this Australian, a writer fellow who had moved into our area. Small town news spreads fast. We both lived in the charming, little, seaside town of Malibu – before it became the enclave of the rich and famous. It was a part of southern California's history, having been at one time a single ranch of some size – twenty-seven miles along the Pacific Coast, to be exact. I noticed Colin's unique and rather unusual saddle. "That's an Aussie stock saddle, mate," he told me with what I would come to find was a requisite grin. We rode along together for quite a while, and he explained the nature of the saddle's origins. We continued our chat until all of a sudden Colin looked at me and stated flatly, "Gotta go, mate, hold onto your horse." Apparently he was late for something or simply decided it was time to run – and off he went, leaving the other riders in the party grabbing reins and saddle cantles, trying to control horses that wanted to follow. It was classic Dangaard, I would find. Make an entrance, but above all, know when to leave – and leave with style.

Colin and I rode a lot together. He especially liked to ride when every other normal human would rather be sitting in front of a warm fire, like on dark and rainy nights. One evening I received a phone call from Colin, and all he said was, "Bill, we're gonna ride, mate, it's raining, it's peeeerrrfect!" I gulped. "Are you kidding? It's pouring!"

"Naw, Bill, it's just a mist, and the footing is still good." His voice trailed off.

Well, I was younger then, and my wife, Kristin, always loved Colin's rides, so off we went. Now, I must tell you Colin's "Night Rides" are never intended to be a walk on the trail. Colin *never* walked on the trail. So, here's the scene: It's about nine thirty in the evening, and Colin has saddled several of his hunt horses with Australian stock saddles. (Note: Colin's horses are a reflection of their owner. They like to go, fast. They are more top-end, fueled dragster-types than hang-your-legs trail-types.) Kristin and I, along with Colin, climbed on and headed for what seemed more of a small deer trail that led away behind his house in the Malibu Mountains. It was dark – really dark, like night, and oh yes, it was *pouring*. So, we're off.

I don't know if it was two or six hours later when we returned to his barn, but considering the speed we were going most of the time, we could have easily run fifty miles. The only tip-off was the number of cliffs we ran along – in the dark, in the rain.

"What a great little jog," he said over his shoulder as he unsaddled the horses.

Jog? I thought, as I limped back to the pickup. But, that was classic Colin. You knew going in, doing something with him would be memorable.

Colin's connection to that Aussie saddle was more than just nationalistic pride. He literally introduced the United States to Aussie-style and Aussie riding with his company, the Australian Stock Saddle Company, which he started from his den in 1979. At the time, I owned an advertising agency, and he asked me to help him launch his Australian revolution in the United States. At this time, his day job was as an internationally syndicated newspaper columnist – oh, did I forget to mention that? Colin, it seems, had quite a skill convincing celebrities all over the world to give him interviews when they wouldn't speak to other journalists. Colin was quite the convincer – imagine that.

As a businessman, Colin has special skills as well. I recall going to a Denver trade show with him when he started marketing his *Australian Whip* video and oilskin coats. In Australia, it seems, bands of horses and wild cattle are driven with the sound of a whip cracking, and so the ability to crack one's whip while on horseback is a treasured indigenous ability in the great Outback of Down Under. In order to show his capability with a whip and to validate his video's authority, he needed a gullible volunteer to hold a cigarette in his mouth. Who better than the ad guy he's trusting? Right. As I mounted the stage of the WESA Market in Denver, I wondered what kind of corrective surgery I would need. Was my face covered on my insurance?

I didn't need to worry. He never missed. Three cigarettes later and an unending number of chopped celery stalks held in both hands, all to the sound of *Rawhide*, and I was done. When he turned at the end of the long runway as I was departing, he couldn't help himself, so, with a horizontal cut, he sliced the whip over the heads of dignitaries seated at the foot of the stage. Heads ducked. Wine glasses froze in hand. An orchid center-table display shuddered. On the way back, Colin laid the big whip down between the runway and the seated audience to give the whip more "fall." Of course, a photographer was there snapping pictures – until he fell back into a table. (The photographer would later complain his right ear was not doing well.) By the time Colin got to the curtain, security was there, and they removed him in such a way that his feet were no longer on the floor. "I just don't get it," said Colin over his shoulder. "I missed that photographer by a full six inches!" It was 1987. That night, Colin owned the place. People still talk about it. He never performed in Denver again.

It may have been Colin's "requisite grin," but the take here is a man who never gives up on what – or who – he believes in. Colin believes in Emma Armbrust. She is for him the one who defines what writer Tom McGuane said of the special relationship some humans have with horses: "Those who love horses are impelled by an ever-receding vision, some enchanted transformation through which the horse and the rider become a third, much greater thing." Emma has not forgotten our "proximity to animals." A proximity that so many chose to leave behind in the last century, running headlong into the future and leaving the help of animals in the fields behind for tractors and combines. We didn't know, as Bill Kittredge wrote, "we let the shadows of the clouds pass us by." We lost a part of ourselves as animals.

It is apparent in this fast-paced, instant-message world we live in now, that Colin's Emma came not just from his mind, but also from a special place in his heart.

After you read *Talking with Horses*, Emma will find a special place in your heart as well. What you'll read is a story of sensitivity and learning. That things are not always as they seem. That patience is a worthy virtue, and that truth and trust are values eternal. What we have here through Colin's enthusiasm and capability is a story that has come from a lifelong love of horses and his ability to craft his words. From knowing his characters' hearts. From taking the time to listen and to learn.

Emma is a reminder that it's not too late for the rest of us. She reminds me of lines from a Simon and Garfunkel song from the 1960s:

Slow down, you move too fast,
You've got to make the morning last.

Bill Reynolds
Santa Ynez, California

Many made this book possible, including the following:

Cindy Tansin, who got sick of me talking about it and insisted I write it. She would not take "too busy" for an answer. Then she held my hand through rewrites.

Neil Davies, one of greatest horse trainers Australia has produced; for his inspiration and encouragement.

Liz Humphreys and Scarlet Walker, each the age of Emma, my lead character. They helped me connect.

Bonnie Bjehle, who recognizes a fine horse and a good sentence when she sees either.

Marlene Smith, who has an ear for a good story and helped me improve on this one.

Jane Lee Beard, who got the big picture and helped me with the details.

Dr. Henry Curry, a physician and remarkable horseman, who guided me most skillfully on matters of medicine, the human brain, and the electromagnetic energy that connects all living creatures.

Derryn Hinch of Australia, my faithful friend for most of five decades. We wrote together as journalists all our lives. He gave me enormous encouragement and told me at my kitchen table, "Write this, you fool! It's in your head!"

Melissa Nocar, for whom typos glow in the dark.

Susan Garber, for intellectual input and providing clues to story flow.

My brother Lawrence, an Outback horseman, who inspired me years ago, in a place long ago and far away. My other brothers: John, an incredible storyteller; and my younger brother Stephen, who followed me as a writer. And my elder sister Camelia, for leading our family; and my sister Rowena, for her encouragement; and my younger sister Daphne, who has worked in my garden and taught me how to smell the roses.

And then there is Kay, who bought me my first horse in America, a polo pony named Kelly. He was no brumby, but he could have been. Kelly was fast and sure.

Stefanie Ward, anthropologist, who guided me on matters of history and dates.

Bob Bryers of Florida for his invaluable promotional input.

And my loving wife, Linda, now deceased who went through my every crazy adventure.

Printed in the United States
By Bookmasters